DEAR FUTURE

Other Books by
Fred D'Aguiar

Fiction
THE LONGEST MEMORY

Poetry
MAMA DOT
AIRY HALL
BRITISH SUBJECTS

Plays
A JAMAICAN AIRMAN FORESEES HIS DEATH

DEAR FUTURE

FRED D'AGUIAR

AVON BOOKS ◆ NEW YORK

AVON BOOKS
A division of
The Hearst Corporation
1350 Avenue of the Americas
New York, New York 10019

First Avon Books Trade Printing: February 1998

AVON TRADEMARK REG. U.S. PAT. OFF. AND IN OTHER COUNTRIES, MARCA REGISTRADA, HECHO EN U.S.A.

Printed in the U.S.A.

OPM 10 9 8 7 6 5 4 3 2 1

This novel bears no relation to any places or persons living or dead. Any resemblance is entirely coincidental. I owe a large debt and insufficient gratitude to my editors Jonathan Burnham and Erroll McDonald, my agent Jane Bradish-Ellames, and to Debbie Dalton as always.

For my brothers—

Gregory, Patrick, Andrew, John, Godfrey and James

. . . my mother who really fathered me . . .

George Lamming

Each of us now held in his arms what he had been for ever seeking and what he had eternally possessed.

Wilson Harris

Contents

I

Dreams from

the Republic of Nightmares

Axe and Anancy

R ED HEAD GOT his name and visionary capacity at age nine when he ran behind an uncle chopping wood and caught the back of the axe on his forehead. His uncle, Beanstalk, feeling the reverberations of a soft wood as it yielded to the blade he'd swung back, looked over his shoulder and saw his favourite nephew half-run, half-walk in a wobbly line, do an about-turn, then flop to the ground in a heap. This was the uncle who, when leading a party hunting for the unbelievably sweet young shoots of coconut plants they'd christened 'growee', began to cross a trench on a log that bucked and flung him off, and who, as everyone scattered and fought to climb the nearest tree, lassoed the log's head and tail before the word 'alligator' had formed on anyone's lips.

The child saw red. Red in the earth and clouds and sky, a red dye making visible the air he could only feel until now and drink too, in confirmation of all he felt, red, in the trees and in the ripe fruit and red behind his shut eyes. Red, then black. Beanstalk dearly wanted the whole thing to be a mischievous joke. Like the time his nephew emptied a half-bottle of rum in one long headback slake and tumbled headfirst down the thirty-eight steps from the house into the back yard in such a state of absolute relaxation that he didn't incur so much as a graze. Something made the uncle stare at the boy's forehead as if he were watching a miniature screen. The ruptured screen resembled a door blown off its hinges. Out stepped a white body of fluid in one boneless move. As if surprised by the sudden recognition that it was naked, the nubile body gathered about itself a flowing red gown which ran in ceaseless yards, covering all of the boy's face in seconds.

Beanstalk dropped the axe, produced a scream that shook the birds like gravity defying fruits from the trees, bolted in a complete circle round the reddening heap of his nephew, then collapsed next to him. The shriek that emptied the trees also woke the house sleeping to the grandfather clock of his axe splitting wood. Doors and shuttered windows sprang open. So many souls materialised from the house, it was as if the scream were a foot that had stepped on an ant nest. Another uncle, younger brother to the one now prone, was the first to reach them. He leapt from the window he looked out of, one floor up, while everyone else took the more conventional route down the stairs. He ran from one body to the next, settling on the smallest and bloodiest since it looked most in need. He opened Red Head's mouth. It was empty. 'Find his tongue,' he shouted between gorging air and expelling it into Red Head's mouth. Cousins and nephews scrambled around the area hunting for a rubbery organ, caked with the recent lunch of roti and curry. Beanstalk stirred, raised his head in the direction of the unconscious nephew he was sure he'd unwittingly beheaded, since his last image of him was of a headless chicken running around, and fainted again. The child had turned as pale as a cloud. Blood drained from him. Then, as if his body did not like the idea of becoming white, it darkened into progressively deeper shades of blue, like the brewing of a storm.

It dawned on the uncle giving resuscitation (more like lightning than a dawning) that the air he was blowing into his nephew's mouth was serving merely to bloat the boy's cheeks; he was playing the instrument of his nephew's face, exhaling into its geometry as he was taught but without

4

success: the child had swallowed his tongue. A neat swipe by the uncle's index finger cleared Red Head's windpipe. Red Head coughed and gasped. The storm that was whipping itself up behind his eyelids evaporated. Instead of blue sky and daylight greeting his opened eyes, he looked up through a pool of red. He saw figures move in slow motion through this red liquid. He identified one of the figures in this parade behind the screen of his forehead as himself. The other was a presidential figure dressed entirely in purple riding a white stallion. Both the President's purple regalia and the white hide and mane of the horse resisted the red stain that permeated the tilted field of Red Head's perspective. Red Head was perched on a russet horse with a draughts board flying in the air between him and the President. Though both horses were in full gallop, the entire scene was undisturbed and the two concentrated on the board as if they were in an airless drawing room instead of sprinting on horseback near the red rim of surf on a red beach.

Next, in this private parade, came a man wrecked by polio. His arms and shoulders were huge and barred and striped with muscles, in shocking contrast to his shrivelled, bony waist and matchstick legs. This broken man was riding a bicycle twice his size. He rode to the end of a jetty and dived off his bike directly into the sea. The wheels of the fallen bike spinning on greased ball bearings and the ticking of the sprocket, with no rider in sight, made it look like the scene of a suicide. The broken man did not sink as one might expect, but zoomed away fluently, his pointed rugby ball of a head floating on the water, his arms rotating like twin propellers, his body submerged like the hull of a ship.

The third image was that of a kite flying without a hand to guide it. A long S-shaped tail made of coins strung together waved under the kite's slow pendulum swing. Both sides of the coins appeared to be a portrait of the same face. A noise akin to the lowest note from a baritone saxophone came from the kite's tongue as the wind blasted it. Under the hard gaze of the sun the kite seemed to be a rainbow in the sky. Each part of the child-high frame, modelled in the shape of a giant hand, was covered in paper of a different primary colour.

All three passed: purple President, broken man and kite. 'There were four,' piped a small, insistent voice. Red Head cut in quickly, 'No, three. I should know. Now get out of my head, you're trespassing.' The little voice obeyed, dissolving with a puff. Film on the projector ran out, leaving a tilted, pitch-black screen as Red Head plummeted into unconsciousness.

Granny was the last one out the door. She appeared to float down towards the commotion as a breeze rushing up the stairs fingered its way under her floor-length dress, causing it to billow like a sail up to her hips, where the muscled breeze gripped her, raised her off her feet and bore her down the stairs, even though the dress was as heavy as the cloth of flour sacks that had been ripped out, dyed and stitched into a simple, tentlike design to sit on her six-foot frame, covering her bones in utilitarian fashion, warding off the heat and retaining pockets of cool air, its pleated fringes used for mopping perspiration from her brow, its dark colour disguising the sweat patches under her arms from her constant meanderings of toil that defined her day and that of the house and everyone in it from sunrise to sunset.

The whirlpool of uncles, aunts, nephews and cousins surrounding Red Head and Beanstalk parted before the grandmother the second she reached its perimeter and closed behind her again as she made her way to its still centre. She knelt beside Red Head. Worry traversed her face, like the shadow of an aeroplane rippling across a field, and disappeared, as if denied permission to settle on it. Granny plastered a dam of a poultice in the split on his forehead and stemmed the tide of blood. Next she turned to Beanstalk,

6

raised his head in her right hand, delicately, as if holding a precious crystal to the light, and with the open palm of her left hand delivered two slaps to his face, one to each cheek, in rapid strokes. Beanstalk sat bolt upright. She returned her attention to Red Head, pulling from her apron the long white flag of a bandage which she used to strap the poultice in place. Red Head groaned. Whispers that Beanstalk might have been spellbound by a pernicious strain of guava circulated among the children.

Wheels was the natural choice to ride the big, black, fixed-wheel bike the five miles to the hospital with his patient balanced on the crossbar. Had it not been lunchtime, they would have used the mule and cart for an ambulance. But the mule was out grazing and would have taken too long to round up, cajole into a harness, strap to the cart and whip from a trot to a full gallop.

Wheels sat on the bicycle with his left foot on the pedal. The saddle was so high the toes of his right foot just reached the ground. He opened his right arm to receive the dazed Red Head and steadied the handlebar with his left. There was a slowness in the way he propped the slumped child on the crossbar, allowing the lolling head to cradle in the crook between his left shoulder and neck. He inclined his head so that the side of his jaw braced the child's head where it rested against him. Once he'd grabbed the handlebar with his right hand, with Red Head's legs draped over his arm, he nodded to no one and everyone that he was ready.

'Give me a push,' were his parting words. His two brothers, the big-headed Bounce and a tearful Beanstalk, gave him the initial running start he required. Wheels broke into an immediate sprint, pulling away from them. A trail of sand from the red road fanned out and up. Everyone looked away and shielded their faces. Wheels, Red Head and the bicycle were lost in the voluminous cloud that followed the road out of town as if a route had been predetermined for their tornado. When the storm brewed by Wheels swooped round the corner and could still dimly be seen above the houses and the trees, only then did the twenty-six uncles, aunts, nephews and cousins with Grandmother dismantle the human roadblock they'd erected across the road.

They had been oblivious to the honking of horns by tractors and the ringing of a dozen bicycle bells that had merged into a huge alarm clock some sleeping giant was ignoring. They had blocked out the church-summoning loudness of the bells on carts, mooing cattle on the drive to the abattoir or market, and bleating sheep. Sheep had gotten mixed with cows, some of whom had butted and kicked them. The minders of both quarrelled among themselves and gesticulated at anyone whose eye they managed to catch, as if to say, 'What did I do to deserve this?'

Jammed behind all these were the big-axled, sixteen-wheeled, fuming, growling, articulated trucks, which reputedly never stopped for anyone or anything they hit. Laden down with their excess payload of rock, sand, wood, broken bottles, tar, water, new billiard cues carved from smoke-cured greenheart wood watered by the Orinoco, billiard balls made from the ground bones of the manatee, food, mainly basmati rice, known throughout the interior and even among the Waiyaku of the upper reaches of the Amazon as the best rice for boiling with coconut milk, and fuel from the oil fields of Surinam, they were all destined for the thousand-strong road gang stationed outside the capital. The road gang was rumoured to be paving the sand road with seamless bitumen, the result so smooth an aeroplane could land or take off on it. These men travelled at a quarter of a mile a day, accompanied by a colony of Chinese and Kashmiri cooks, Ghanaian seamstresses and laundresses, barbers whose ancestors were from Karachi and the ancient city of Lahore, Cuban doctors and nurses who relied on the

surrounding vegetation for whatever medicines they prescribed, and Amerindian prostitutes who floated between
four ad hoc bars: one for cocktails, run by an Italian from the
north corner of Lake Garda; another peddling frothy beers
and managed by a 600-pound German wrestler;
a third dealing exclusively in wines pressed from grapes
grown in the Dordogne but owned by a male couple from
Brittany with their own language and swearwords for
anyone who dared to tell them they should speak patois; and
a fourth, specialising in the overproof spirits of the Wind-
ward Islands of the Caribbean, run by four Jamaicans. The
Jamaicans also managed the two coffee huts whose beans
came from the Blue Mountains of their island's heartland
and were as valuable as gold bullion; in fact, used as such by
the government on more than one occasion to pay the
contractors who had lost faith in the bonds issued to them
and threatened to withhold their expertise unless the
treasured beans were made available to them in several
hundred bushels ready for export. Added to these were a
comedy theatre of six Englishmen in their late forties who
were foremen of the road gang during the day but whose
commedia dell' arte at night consisted of cross-dressing with
coconut shells as breasts, kente cloth from Accra for
elaborate headdresses and moccasins from Oklahoma,
drawing catcalls, wolf whistles and applause from the same
men they had been ordering around a few hours earlier and
would be in charge of again after a night's sleep; a cinema
that was really only a projector and a white sheet stitched to
two poles for outdoor screening on dry, insect-ridden
nights, which showed Hindi films made in the cavernous
studios of Bombay, with their countless love songs which
the men committed to their hearts and mouthed during their
labour; and an American supermarket with fifty varieties of
cereal, all under tarpaulin, which competed with the trading
stalls set up on carts owned by Venezuelans. Spontaneous

stick fights, stone throwing, arm wrestling, boxing and cricket matches would break out between the rowdy or sporting contingent in the road gang and the inhabitants of whatever locality the red road they were converting to an airstrip happened to pass. Soldiers and police, tax collectors and moneylenders, lawyers and psychics, were always camping nearby, some to maintain law and order, others to corrupt it, in this nomadic city trundling towards the house where Red Head lived with his twenty-six relatives and Granny and Grandad, all of whom swore they would not let the road gang's city enter Ariel.

'There were four.'

Red Head woke to the small voice he'd banished from inside his head what seemed like only a second earlier, but from his surroundings must have been hours, perhaps days ago.

'There will be red, then there will be black.'

The voice increased in volume as light intensified in the room. Red Head thought of lifting his arm and flattening into an asterisk whatever it was on his forehead that bugged him, but his arms were two cement blocks by his side, obedient to a will other than the one he mustered.

'You will listen. There were four.'

The voice did a thumping march across his forehead. His eyes watered. A flashbulb flickered though his lids were pressed tight. Each flicker was triggered by a syllable from that voice. Each syllable delivered a hammer blow to his nerves. And every strand of his nervous system seemed strung into a wet mop being wrung tighter and tighter by two powerful hands.

'Red, then black. I know you can hear.'

There had been a fourth image in the parade behind his skull witnessed moments after the bolt of lightning from the axe. But what he saw had scared him so much he had censored it, cut it from the film he had viewed and put it at the back of a bottom drawer in an attic room he'd locked with a key he'd thrown far away.

'There were four. Red, then black.'

The voice grew to a deafening boom. Light flickered so fast the flashes became a glare. Red Head felt the water run from his eyes and collect in his ears. He allowed the attic room to surface. The hands that wrung the mop released their grip immediately and allowed the strands to shake loose. The flicker behind his eyes lessened to something a little slower than the second hand of a clock.

'There were four,' he admitted to himself.

'All right!' the small torturer's voice shrieked, accelerating the flickering and the thumps for two drawn-out seconds before they became a dull, intermittent ache once more. Red Head conjured a picture of the attic door and willed it to open. 'Open sesame,' were the only words he could think of. A career at picking locks suggested itself to him but he was swift to push it to the edge of his mind, afraid he might invite again the voice that made him cry like a baby. Just as he was about to open the drawer and reach in to retrieve whatever he'd hidden there, he made one last effort to banish from his head the attic, the bottom drawer and, he hoped, the pernicious little voice as well, by summoning a fact.

'Ariel, formerly Percival, Cooperative Republic Village number – One windowless government school run by a teacher with a class of forty-nine, ages ranging from six to sixteen. One rum shop. One baker. Countless guava, guinep, sapodilla, mango, downs, tamarind and coconut trees . . .'

The intruder in Red Head's skull, put there, he thought, by the surgeon who had stitched the opening made by the axe, resumed his torture of Red Head.

'There were four! Red, then black!'

The slow flicker went straight to a glare, followed by a thumping across his forehead so rapid it would have made an hour pass in a few seconds if it had been keeping time. Again, two big hands gathered the straggly mop of Red Head's nervous constitution and twisted it. Tears stung Red Head's eyes. Instead of giving in to the voice and attic and contents of the bottom drawer, Red Head summoned more facts to help him in his fight, this time a story the teacher told to his class one rainy day at recess when they were all stuck inside and rain blew in the port-holes that served as windows.

'Anancy the spider had one hand of bananas which he brought home to his wife and four children for their first meal that day – '

'There were four, damn you!'

'How many bananas make a hand? He gave each of his children one banana. How many did he have left? Anancy offered the last banana to his wife. She refused to accept it. She begged him to eat it. She said he needed the strength to go out and find the next meal – '

'Four! Red, then black!' The little intruder emphasised each word by jumping four times on the wound on Red Head's forehead. A near-colourless fluid began to seep out despite the ten tight stitches.

'Anancy the spider insisted until his wife accepted. They sat round the table. Anancy took his usual place. His empty plate stood out next to the plates with bananas that belonged to his wife and children. Anancy's wife cut her banana in half and put one half on her husband's plate. A small light appeared in Anancy's eyes – '

The little devil repeated his athletic exercise. 'Four!' Jump. 'Red!' Jump. 'Then!' Jump. 'Black!' Jump. Red Head bit his tongue but found the interruption only served to make him want to get to the end of his Anancy story.

'Anancy looked at the banana on the plate of his eldest son. His son followed his father's gaze, cut a third off his banana and put it on his father's plate. Anancy's eyes grew wider and brighter as his gaze travelled to the plate of his second child. She too saw his eyes and did exactly what her brother had done. She cut a third off her banana and put it on her father's plate. How much banana has Anancy collected so far?'

The little devil jumped on the wound and began to twist on it as he sang, 'There were four! Red, then black!' to a rock-and-roll tune. Red Head coiled and squirmed, pulled at his bed sheets and cried but continued his Anancy story.

'Anancy's third and fourth children followed their father's gaze as it crept up to their plates, then they copied their brother's and sister's example by slicing a third off their bananas and placing the pieces on their father's full plate. Anancy's eyes grew so wide his face became two headlights on full beam. How many bananas did Anancy end up with?'

'There!' Twist. 'Were!' Twist. 'Four!' Twist and jump.

The diminutive devil was ankle-deep in blood, ruptured flesh and severed nerves. He paused to look at Red Head. He saw that the boy's face was a series of crags and ridges, while his teeth were bared (though no sound escaped his wide mouth) and bloody from a bitten tongue. Pint Size, the name that occurred to Red Head for his tormentor, stepped out of the wound, shook the muck from his boots and settled down next to the suppurating mass in a half-lotus. Red Head allowed the door to the attic to swing open. He reached to the back of the bottom drawer. The forbidden fourth image flickered to life. Red Head was shuddering, yet he was covered in sweat. He found it hard to bring the image on the screen into focus. Whatever it was, it looked much like the kite of the previous image. Red Head thought it might be a mistake, that it was indeed the third image being replayed, but before he could do anything to sharpen what he saw so poorly into something recognisable, the light faded, then reddened, then went black. Pint Size punched the air with his fist, considered jumping into Red Head's wound again to twist for a bit, but thought better of it, and said very quietly into Red Head's left ear, so that Red Head heard even though he had slipped into unconsciousness, 'Another day, Axe-features. There will be another day.'

'The doctor said he had to strap your hands to your side.'
   'What did I ever do to him?'
'He said you destroyed his neat stitches.'
'Why would I do a stupid thing like that?'
'Delirium.'
'You let a strange man tie me down and sew me up?'
   Wheels smiled because this was the Red Head he knew and loved, with a tongue in his mouth more like a whip for one so young. He pedalled as if out on an afternoon jaunt. Even this far inland a cool sea breeze nudged them from behind. At the S-bend, on Ariel's outskirts, two police motorcycles pulled up and waved Wheels to the side of the road. Soon a black limousine approached. Wheels thought of covering Red Head's bandaged head to protect it from the dust the car would raise as it flew past but Red Head wanted to see. Instead of splashing red sand in their faces and disappearing in a cloud, the car slowed to a crawl. A window in the back seat glided down and sprouted an arm, then a face, masked in a pair of silver-tinted sunglasses with massive lenses – just like the ones his father wore propped up on his skull when indoors and dropped over his eyes with a sharp nod as he ducked into sunlight. The arm waved, the face smiled. Red Head saw himself reflected twice in the sunglasses with two astounded copies of Wheels trying to salute and keep the two Red Heads stable on the crossbar at the same time. When the eyes behind the glasses made four with Red Head's eyes and winked, Red Head winked back. The police motorcycles accelerated away, followed by the limousine, whose open window retrieved the arm and face and glided up, shutting out the sun and dust.

14

'Did you see yourself in double karate-chopping the air?'

'The thought of three of you frighten me more than him. One bad enough.' Both laughed.

The encounter with the President spurred on the legs of Wheels. He raised himself off the saddle and made a dust cloud of his own to rival the President's limousine. Red Head leaned with Wheels into both corners of the S-bend. His bandaged head felt weightless. He closed his eyes and listened to the bicycle tyres eating up the yards of sand between them and the house. Each time Wheels pressed down on the pedals Red Head heard the teeth of a saw being pulled and pushed through wood. Soon the sawing lost the little pauses between each stroke as Wheels reached a sprint. It became the continuous whirr of propellers. Wind sang in their ears. They were flying. The frequent little bumps were turbulence.

Wheels drew up in front of the house. Everyone came out. Someone shouted, 'Axe-man back!' Beanstalk lifted Red Head off the bike, hugged him and showered him with apologies. Beanstalk's head was inches above the six-foot paling fence. He loved to impress the children by vaulting it in a peculiar backwards dive. As Beanstalk bounced along the path from the road to the house with Red Head in his arms, the boy rested his chin on his uncle's right shoulder and tried to count the individual slats of the paling fence as they bobbed up and down.

'Boy, I thought I chop off your head!'

His uncle's casual strides were so long Red Head fell further and further behind in his count. He skipped some palings until his eyes drew level with his uncle's legs but found as he resumed counting that he immediately fell behind again.

'You make a big man like me faint!'

Instead of skipping a few palings as before, Red Head gave up counting and watched the pattern of light and shade made by the spaces between the palings and his uncle's deft pace.

'Nothing ever scare me so!'

'I sorry I make you faint, Uncle. I sorry I scare you.'

'Boy, I wish it was my head that axe clap.'

Beanstalk gave Red Head a little squeeze. His nephew squeezed him back.

'Guava had nothing to do with it.'

'I know, Uncle.'

He climbed the few steps to the porch with Red Head in his arms and met his mother at the door. He handed Red Head over to her. Whereas Beanstalk was solid and hot, Red Head's grandmother felt soft and cool. Beanstalk had smelled of the sun; Granny, on the other hand, smelled of soap.

'I see the President, first in purple on a white stallion, then in a limousine. He had dark glasses like Daddy's and I beat him at draughts.'

'You beat everybody at draughts.'

Someone shouted from the yard, 'In your dreams.'

'Ask Wheels.'

Wheels nodded. 'Is true what Red Head saying. I don't know about a white stallion but our great benefactor did pass us in his black limo.'

Not everyone was impressed by the attention Red Head was receiving. Someone who sounded like Red Head's elder brother shouted, 'You're Axe-man now.'

'I am no Axe-man. I is Red Head. He should be Axe-man.' Red Head pointed with his chin to Beanstalk, who looked away with a broad smile. But a second voice, this time belonging to Bounce, the youngest of his three uncles, with a huge head that was harder than a coconut stripped of its husk and who could butt anyone on any part of their body and make them cry without his eyes so much as watering, shouted, 'Is too late, once you get name that is it, Axe-man!'

16

'Go butt down a tree, Hammerhead!'

Bounce shook his concrete block in amusement and delivered a quick rejoinder, 'Your head blunt the axe, not mine!' This raised a big laugh from everyone.

Red Head tried to match the smiling paving stone. 'That same axe would have bounced off your mallethead and chopped Beanstalk!'

There were wolf whistles as everyone prepared for a slanging match. His grandmother turned away from them with him and pulled the door shut behind her. Red Head heard someone shout, 'When is an axe not an axe?' The question made him cork his ears with his fingers. He did not want to hear the reply to a riddle he had no part in solving. But he still caught the raucous laughter that erupted in response to a muffled voice that sounded like his brother's.

'Never mind, child. You still my little Red Head.'

Granny led him into a bedroom designated for his convalescence. He felt giddy. She eased him onto the bed.

'So you saw our President?'

Red Head nodded. He let his head drop onto the cool, white, ironed cotton pillowcase, shut his eyes and pondered when an axe was not an axe. He wished he'd heard the answer because now he would have to make one up.

'He only stop because election coming up.'

'I know, but he stop for just Wheels and me.'

'You don't know, Red Head. We can't afford to have any losers in this election.' Granny put a damp cloth on his bandaged forehead. The cloth's coldness made him suck on the air. His mind emptied of everything except the lime-grove scent and mesmeric cool of the cloth. This strip of cloth was bleached. Though he could not smell it, he could tell from its stark whiteness. And it resembled several others he'd seen drying on the line every few weeks or so but whose function he'd never believed when told by his girlfriend Sten that the cloths were used by the grown women to stem a monthly flow of blood.

'Does that mean that you will bleed?'

'Yes, one day.'

He had changed the subject after a moment's silence and pushed the information to the back of his mind.

'When can I get up, Granny?'

'What do you mean, when can I get up? You just lie down!'

'I was only wondering.'

'Well, you wonder and stay in that bed!'

'All I want is to know.'

'Soon, soon.'

When his mother had gone abroad with his three younger brothers and left him in Ariel with his elder brother, she too had told him soon. She would return soon. That was six months ago. He missed her. She was bony but her skin was soft. She was sweeter than any fruit or flower, whereas Granny carried the odour of soap and, when she'd just brought clothes in off the line, of the sun. At his age every desire was soon. And his father had gone away. Just like that, he'd dived into the hot afternoon, his eyes hidden with a nod just in time to avoid the sun. The last time Red Head had talked with Bash Man Goady about missing their mother, father and brothers, they were having a walk-race to school. His brother was breathless but he'd paused to draw hard on the air and had spoken as if they had been swinging in the hammock at the bottom of the house.

'If you don't think about it, it won't hurt.'

He had taken his brother's advice as a necessary gospel. So far it seemed to work when he was awake, but when he slept all he saw were his three brothers and his mother, just out of earshot of him. And no matter how hard he ran towards them, they always maintained the same distance from him even though they did not move. But his father, who was never in these dreams, was simply gone. Red Head would wake up with his heart pounding, angry and ready to cry, but because he was not alone, he could not cry. The others would see and they'd call him a crybaby and laugh at him.

Red Head woke up to a bowl of soup, three pieces of buttered bread and his friend Raj smiling at him. He sat up in bed and ate fast. The bread was oven-warm. Melted butter had to be balanced on the slice as he lifted it to his face. He inhaled deeply, then took a big bite and chewed with his eyes closed. He drained the bowl of rice and pea soup and would have used his bread to wipe the bowl had Raj not been there. All this time Raj stood and watched him and smiled. Once Red Head was finished, Raj took the tray from his lap and placed it on the floor. Red Head propped himself up some more but his grandmother cast him such a look when she came to collect the empty tray that he slid down under the bedclothes until his head was resting on the pillow again.

'Granny, your soup and bread is the best in the whole wide world.'

'Child, what do you know about the world?'

She rested the back of her hand on his forehead, squinted at the bandage and exited. The hem of her long dress swept the floor clean of any prints she might have left.

'Raj! What you got to tell me?'

'Boy, something boss!'

Raj had a photographic memory for Westerns. He didn't tell you what happened in a film, he showed you. He spoke all the parts and drew an imaginary pistol from an imaginary holster and made a pistol shot with his pursed lips in rough synchronisation to his cocked thumb hitting his pointed index finger. His weak sphincter muscle interrupted his show several times. As a result he tended to shorten any long panning shots or rides into and out of towns. Despite wads of tissue stuffed down his trousers, there remained a

19

permanent wet patch on his crotch. A strong smell of urine emanated from him, earning him the name Pissy-missy. Were it not for this affliction, his Westerns would have made him many more friends. Once Raj got going, the smell around him evaporated and his wet patch vanished. Granny came into the room and opened the window. Raj had got to the point where the star boy, as all the heroic cowboys were called, had an arm pumped full of lead and he was in the process of crawling off to his hideout to be nursed back to health by an Indian woman. Granny placed the back of her hand on Red Head's forehead.

'That's enough for today, Raj. You killing him with all the excitement.'

Raj waved from the door. Granny twitched her nose. Red Head knew it was because of the rancid smell, but he said nothing and did everything in his power not to twitch his nose too. She changed his bandage. Neither spoke. Towards the end of dressing his head, she began to hum a calypso. He knew the words and smiled.

'What tickle you?'

'I know that song. It rude.'

'If you know it rude, you better don't let me catch you singing it.'

Instead of the words to the calypso, the solution to the axe puzzle leapt from his mind onto his tongue like one of those fishes in the trench that sometimes shot clear of the muddy water and ended up on the bank in an epileptic frenzy as they drowned in air.

'Axe! Ask! When is an axe not an axe? When it is a request! When you ask for something!'

'Boy, you too bright for your own good.'

'Can I play draughts with someone? I won't sit up.'

'All right, but only a couple of games, no more.'

Bash Man Goady hovered with the board and the draughts as if waiting for an invitation. They nodded and set about erecting the black and white round pieces on opposing squares. Red Head glanced at Bash Man Goady and caught him scrutinising his damaged forehead out of the corner of his eye.

'Does it hurt?'

'Not a lot.'

'Boy, I never see so much blood in my life.'

'Did you think I was going to die?'

'No. You're a Santos. We're tough.'

They looked at each other and smiled in a rare offering of kindness. The departure, first of their father and then their mother and younger brothers, had driven a wedge between them. Whenever there was a dispute in the house they found themselves on opposing sides. In school they never spoke to each other and when they went on day trips, people were often surprised to learn they were related, never mind brothers. Red Head had overheard his mother trying to explain the rivalry between them to her alarmed mother-in-law, after their first terrible fight at Ariel in which they'd exchanged punches until their eyes were closed.

'I don't know,' she'd said in stubborn bewilderment. 'Is like the second one born too soon when he born at seven months, and the first one feel he get push out of the way.'

His grandmother began to offer some remedy in her usual method of contradicting everything Red Head's mother said or did, but he had heard enough and had already bolted from the kitchen door convinced that his premature appearance into the world was solely responsible for his brother's short temper and grouchy demeanour.

'Hello? Wake up! I said, What's this about beating the President at draughts?'

'Boy, I wash his gall! It was only a dream but it was real as you and me talking now.'

'You think you will win the National Draughts Championships?'

21

'You want me to?'

'What kind of question is that? Of course!'

'I wasn't sure.'

'Look, you is my brother, right? We fight and things, but you is my blood. Put our name on the map!'

Red Head hopped over three of Bash Man Goady's pieces and gained a king.

'Man! I can't play you, you too good!'

Granny came in and from her knitted brows he knew it was time to rest. His brother packed up the game, proffered that rare smile again and left. Granny tucked him in so tightly he had to strain to loosen the sheets. Then she dropped the mosquito net over his bed. To him the net was like the lid of a casket, sealed with him inside. Had the axe been one inch lower to the left or right this would have been his fate; except it would have been dark with less room to manoeuvre. He shuddered. His grandmother's tone was neither admonishing nor sarcastic when she watched his struggle with the sheets and asked him whether he thought he'd turned into a man. He still felt weak and any sudden move made his head throb.

He lost track of the days. Everyone was at school or in the rice fields or minding the cows or attending to the pigs or the chickens or preparing some meal in the kitchen. Everyone was everywhere but in the room with him. They were kind enough to leave him a draughts set but playing against himself only revealed the futility of any attempt to fool or trick his mind. They brought him a slate from school on which he practised his writing, which was better than usual without the teacher looking over his shoulder. He wrote the alphabet with a flourish as if his name consisted of all twenty-six letters, pretending that his chalk was really a quill and that he was signing the Declaration of Independence of his country from British rule or the unification of all the land's seven peoples. He also made up words by haphazardly juxtaposing letters plucked from his head or suggested by a portion of the wall that had caught his eye. Some mornings he'd be dreaming, something he couldn't recount when awake, and the smell of Granny's baked bread that filled the house at dawn would work its way into his dream, causing his mouth to water, stirring the desire for food and nudging him from sleep with its promise of fresh bread, melted butter and tea.

Raj visited once more, armed with the story of a new Western he'd seen. His sound effects of gunfights involving up to a dozen gunslingers with an array of six-shooters and rifles produced foam at the corners of his mouth, imbued with a urinous air acrid as sulphur. After Raj departed, Granny opened the window and left in a hurry without a word. Red Head was sure she was holding her breath throughout. Bash Man Goady looked in now and again too, sometimes with a message from Sten, other times for a quick game of draughts. Grandad's visits were the most important of all. He'd sit on the end of the bed and ask Red Head to imagine a draughts board on the sheet between them. Then he would talk what he called 'tactics' with his grandson. Red Head never saw Grandad leave because without fail he'd fall asleep at some point during these tactical lectures. Grandad kept returning so Red Head reasoned that he couldn't have minded.

One morning Granny came in to change his bandage. He sat up. She circled his head with her hand as she unwound the cloth. He thought he was being blessed, but the sign was a circle, not a cross. Somehow the Crucifixion had occurred and the most important motif that had emerged from the event was a circle. He pictured the front of churches and Bibles with a circle on them and light radiating out from the edges of the circles. Perhaps Jesus had been tied to a wheel he had to carry in public to jeers and taunts and then lowered into water repeatedly until he drowned. What about the two

23

thieves? Where would he place them? On two more wheels with all three being lowered head first periodically into the water?

He inclined his head for a new bandage in vain. Granny pointed to the door. Red Head hugged her and headed straight for the voices he could hear splashing in the shell pond. At the pond the others were so pleased to see him, they stopped their game of trying to escape the touch of whoever was the last to be touched and clapped and cheered. Most called him Red Head; a few, Axe-man. He saw reflected in the mirror of the shell pond a path on his forehead much like the red sand road in its wavering but the ten stitches across the gash made it look like a single railway line with sleepers across it. Someone splashed near him and the image shimmered. Now his face softened just as the red sand did after rain when the cars got stuck in it but he knew the road on his forehead would be impervious to water. As he shaped up for a belly-splashing dive, he remembered a finger waving a warning in his face, so close it displaced the air there. He was not to go near the shell pond and get his head wet. He dismissed his dive as a bad idea under the circumstances and waded in. A cool stocking rode up his legs. At crotch level he gasped, pulled in his stomach and straightened to his full height. At chest level he stood still for a moment, allowing the pleasant shock of the ring climbing his body to be warmed by the sun. He swam like a dog, keeping his head high out of the water and paddling his hands below the water in front of him. The others resumed their game. Everyone took care not to splash around him.

There were shells on the bottom, though he could not recall when he had last looked down with his face pressed through the skin of the pond's surface to witness their magnified clarity. He automatically responded to the thought by lowering his chin but checked himself, jerking his head back. His eyes shut out the light and the water went very cold. The mirror of the pond he now located in the sky. According to this logic all he needed to do to see the bed of the shell pond was to raise his eyes. The sheet of lightning he'd missed for weeks struck and blackened his sight. He swallowed. Copper sprang to mind. Trees and sky were shells laid out on this black background for inspection. The whole arrangement was tilted at an angle. He took this as an invitation for him to ponder its detail.

'There will be red, then there will be black. The red sand road will be a river of blood. The river will dry but the red sand will not reappear. A hard, black road will run through the heart of the land.' The small, unshakeable voice was familiar to Red Head. He struggled to focus on the shells but they remained blurred. The tilted display receded from him or he from it.

The others did not miss Red Head. They'd grown accustomed to playing around him and then had proceeded to ignore him. Beanstalk was watching the children playing in the shell pond from a first-floor window he habitually sat beside as he smoked and talked to whoever was in the kitchen. He sounded as if he was shouting at someone because the entrance to the kitchen was at the far end of the room. Perhaps it was hard to register the fact that one of the heads, the least frantic of them, had lowered itself in the water and had not surfaced for some time. He stopped shouting in mid-sentence and placed his cigarette on the edge of the table with the lit end hanging but without taking his eyes off the pond. Whoever was in the kitchen heard him exclaim, 'Jesus!', and if they had had time to enter the room he was in, they would have seen him leap from the window to the ground and run at the fence that was a few inches short of his six feet five inches and take the fence in a backward flip which he simply pointed into a dive as he entered the shell pond. When Beanstalk surfaced, Red Head was in his arms. He depressed Red Head's stomach and blew air into his lungs. Red Head spluttered.

A small, close, truly wicked voice whispered, 'There were four.'

Later that day Beanstalk carried Red Head across the field of tall razor grass separating Grandmother's house from the mud hut of the reclusive Miss Metage, who administered natural remedies for children's aches and pains. Her hands had delivered Red Head's youngest brother, whose sudden birth was brought on when his mother chased Bash Man Goady to lock him in the brush pen for his bad behaviour. The exertion, though successful since she was the fastest sprinter in the village, nevertheless made her double up with labour pains. The children called Miss Metage Ole Higue because they were sure she flew on a broom at night and sucked the life out of babies in their cots. Whenever they saw her they ran from her, all except Red Head's youngest brother, and she reserved her smile just for him.

She pointed to a rug on the floor of her mud hut. The second Beanstalk released him, Red Head sat up and peered at the stooped, short body of the woman. He was afraid to look into her eyes. She motioned at Red Head to lie on his back but he obeyed only when Beanstalk raised his eyebrows at him. She passed a string over an open flame burning in a small, spherical metal dish and allowed the wax running off the string to fall on her open palm as she moved, swiftly for her years, from the one small table in the hut to where Red Head lay. Her hand came away from the bottom of the string and the hot wax dripped on Red Head's bare chest. He bawled. Beanstalk winced but he knew it was fear more than pain that had caused the child to scream. When she asked Beanstalk to hold the whimpering Red Head as still as possible, the child's sobbing renewed. 'This will not hurt.' She reached for the metal dish with the single flame. Shielding the flame with her hand and body so that Red

Head could only see her back as she drew near and stooped next to him, she thrust it at his eyes. Red Head tried to pull his head back but his uncle's grip was too strong. He clamped his eyelids and saw lightning. His tongue was instantly coated with copper. 'Let him go.'

Beanstalk eased his twitching nephew onto the mat and looked at Miss Metage for an explanation. But she was busy placing a folded piece of cloth under the child's head and peering into his mouth to ensure he had not bitten or swallowed his tongue. When Red Head's shuddering stopped and he opened his eyes but did not seem to know where he was, Miss Metage took the cap off a dark bottle, waved the open neck near his nose and his head cleared. She held the bottle at arm's length from herself and Red Head, and Beanstalk took it and replaced the cap.

'Don't screw it too tight or I'll have to call you next time I want to open it.' She tried to mop Red Head's brow but he recoiled. When she smiled at him and tried again, he let her. 'You had a fit. You are young, you might grow out of it. Never stare at the sun or any flickering bright light. Always keep a lump of sugar in your pocket in case you feel hungry. Never stand on your head or dive head-first into water. Avoid sudden noise and don't let anyone hit you on the head again.' She looked at Beanstalk when she said the part about avoiding knocks to the head, and he examined his feet. 'Why you never bring the boy to me when you chop his head? Whoever stitch this must have been drunk.' She selected a jar from a row lined up against the wall on the floor, lifted a feather in it and daubed Red Head's cut with a brown, viscous liquid. This time he kept his head very still for her. She blew on the cut and it felt cool and the skin around the cut stiffened a little as the liquid dried. It reminded him of how mud felt after he crossed a trench and the mud on his feet went dry. Miss Metage ruffled his hair and broadened her smile and gave him a cake made from pieces of coconut covered in brown sugar.

'Thank you, Ole – Miss Metage.'

Beanstalk gave her two small bags; one contained rice, the other flour.

'Feed him with the heart of young coconut trees. That will mend his mind.' She told Red Head if he blurted 'thank you' once more, he would induce a fit. 'Say howdy to your mother.'

Beanstalk gave him a piggyback along a winding path across the field to their house. Red Head decided never to run from Miss Metage again and never to hide from her and pelt her with the red sand stones that exploded on impact. He asked Beanstalk if she really flew on a broom and turned into a ball of fire in order to get through keyholes to babies' cots. His uncle said Miss Metage wouldn't hurt a fly.

'Boy, it looks like we have to find you some growee.'

'Would that be like trying to find guava?'

'Much easier, I think.'

Red Head speculated whether a fit would hinder or help his game in the coming draughts championships. Beanstalk was sure fits would prove useful, if Red Head could summon them at will.

'What if I could touch someone's head during a fit and pass it on to them?'

'Or when you touch them you could read their thoughts!'

'Now that's what I call power!'

Singh v. Singh 1

'CUSHEE CUSHEE MANAY, cushee cushee manoe, bolo bolo masee, ackee jai jai jai.' As yet unbroken voices wailed the Hindi film's signature tune. They skipped home in the dark, flanked by singing aunts and uncles. Another fortnightly village screening was over. Red Head had seen Raj there. They'd squatted on the grass with their arms around each other's shoulders for the duration of the film. Ariel's next big event had been announced, the appearance of the great wrestler Singh, who was over from India on a national tour, and the adults in Raj's family had waved goodbye to Red Head's aunts and uncles.

Local representatives of both political parties had agreed not to canvass at the film show or distribute any leaflets or shout any slogans. This had been adhered to with diligence. News of Singh's event caused a few disgruntled whispers among the government supporters who felt that it was purely political that he was appearing in Ariel so close to an election. But the film had been so good almost everyone was talking about it as they dispersed.

Red Head made it clear that he liked the colourful saris on the women and the drumming. His brother stated what he would and wouldn't do if he got hold of the leading actress. She had the biggest, blackest eyes the children had ever seen, reminiscent of the youngest of their three brothers gone overseas. Red Head became quiet. The memory drained his high spirits. His brother nudged him. Red Head smiled. Soon, soon.

Voices were lowered on the stretch of road outside old Sabbatic's house. They all knew he drank methylated spirits, paraffin and other petroleum derivatives. They believed the rumour, circulated for as long as they could remember, that in a brawl between a half dozen men and him over the attentions of an Amerindian woman in a Georgetown whorehouse, he was chopped with cutlasses several times but the blades bounced off his body.

The house was dark and quiet. There was none of his customary singing and crying, no vituperative cursing and throwing of his few chairs and pots and pans around the house (some of which flew out of the house's many openings to the moon and the stars and slanted rain) and no tongues of flame expectorated by Sabbatic when he couldn't stand the taste of the fuel that consumed him and so took it in his mouth and huffed and puffed it into a twelve-foot tree of fire. The children's urgent pace subsided when the house became indistinguishable from the wall of darkness that was always exactly behind them.

Red Head's brother wanted an aunty to tell him which could be removed more quickly, a sari or a dress. One aunty swore a dress. She told the story of getting her mother to pass her a dress, how her mother had thrown it at her and she had raised both hands and ducked her head and her arms pushed through the sleeves and her head passed through the top of the dress and the dress settled on her body, all from that throw by her mother. Everyone agreed this was too rare to count. Another aunty argued for the sari on the grounds that it didn't have zips and fasteners and belts and buttons, just ornate yards of cloth arranged on the body to cover the important organs. The boys liked the word 'organ'. Red Head thought it reminded him of the name of a vegetable. An uncle said Organ was the first name of a man in a play written by a Welsh poet whose name was on the tip of his tongue. Someone volunteered Chester. Another shouted

Handel. Yet another Tony. Once the younger children cottoned on to the search for names that echoed body parts, they joined in. Red Head said Brian. This halted proceedings. His brother spelled it out loud, pronounced it slowly, then shouted, 'Brain!' to the delight of the nephews and cousins and uncles and aunts.

Granny met them at the front gate. She said they should shush because Wheels was asleep. Wheels spent his days training hard for the forthcoming First National Cycle Championships organised by the government. They'd seen over the weeks how his training three times a day had doubled the size of his thighs and calves. He ate the most meat and rice in the house. First prize meant an automatic place on the national team which would represent the country in races abroad, instead of those hazardous and gruelling trials where talented riders ended up crippled for life under a pile of careless, 'trying-to-run-before-they-can-walk', as Granny called them, amateurs.

The younger children were not allowed to touch Wheels's bike. If they did, they invited invectives from his two brothers Beanstalk and Bounce (otherwise known as Hammerhead, Mallethead, Shovelfeatures, Spadeforehead, Rocketnoggin, Bulletskull, Coconuthead and Ramrod), who passed their free time polishing the individual spokes, oiling and greasing the chain and gears and examining the ball bearings in the hubs of the wheels for specks of dust. They did everything to the bike except christen it with a name; the right incident that would confer that name just hadn't presented itself.

Everyone sat on the veranda. Red Head and Bash Man Goady helped Granny to bring cups of ice-cooled mauby and corn sticks from the kitchen. A three-quarter moon and the occasional piercing star began to peep from behind clouds. The air was warm and barely moved. If there was a great fan whipping up the air it was far out to sea so that by

31

the time the air had covered the few miles inland its effect was dulled to a feather-tumbling wisp of a movement, detectable only if the tongue were run over the lips. The usual chorus of insects seemed patternless most of the time until the lights of the fireflies coincided with it for what seemed like minutes but could have been only a few seconds. During these moments each light appeared to isolate itself from all the others into a distinct sound from that chorus. Sounds and lights appeared to synchronise, one giving definition to the other, and then, after an age, the two would fall into disarray again. Granny's rocking chair over the loose boards on the veranda added to the chorus of chaos.

Red Head settled in the arms of his aunty with the prehensile feet. He looked up at her face to check that she didn't mind and she smiled. She could thread a needle with her feet (steadying it in her right, guiding the thread through the needle's eye with her left) and suck as much as a mouthful of water from the shell pond into her vagina. She would lift her dress above her waist, wade in waist-deep, contract her facial muscles, wade out, and release the water, which trickled onto the ground and ran down her spread legs. Once someone said she was in fact peeing each time. So she drank nothing for a day, sweated at her chores and did not even swallow her spit. Late that afternoon she walked into the shell pond up to her waist, paused, came out, then stooped over a large cup into which she dropped her usual quota of pond water. She proved irrefutably that it could only have been pond water by her next act: she threw her head back, drained the cup, smacked her lips and exhaled loudly.

Granny's voice punctured the reverie. She said the road was coming. Wheels had met it on his afternoon ride. He was able to pedal so fast the wind stopped him from seeing ahead. He would have to get goggles to ride on that road. Rain ran off it as if it were skin, cows lost their footing and had to be lifted off their stomachs; even goats had to crawl off it on their bellies and into the roadside trench to get back on their feet. Cars flew off it too or ran head-on into each other with a loud kiss. The road was moving at a snail's pace but it would be here as sure as tomorrow would come. The children said they would stone this mad thing and stop it from passing through Ariel. But Granny said the road would bring electricity, more traffic and more people. Electricity would mean they could make their own ice, find a pin on the floor at night, and harvest rice round the clock if they wished.

Red Head wanted to know the colour of this road. His grandmother said black. The word 'black' released a small electrical charge through Red Head's body. He stiffened and sprang to his feet. His cicatrised forehead ached as if the current had completed a circuit and had come to rest there. Copper surfaced on his tongue. He shouted that the road was a bad thing. Everyone hissed at him to be quiet or he would wake Wheels and had that axe blow made him stupid or something, didn't he hear what Granny just said? Red Head stepped over their arms and legs and into the house to the bedroom where he slept with his brother and three cousins and lay down. He tried to keep a patch on the ceiling in focus but the patch seemed to undulate and transform from wood to water. What was keeping the water hanging like a basket up there? He lifted his hand towards it and saw fingers and a wrist that seemed to bear no connection to his body. The hand was dabbling in that floating patch of water but not a single sensation of his hand in water registered with him. Might this be a prelude to a fit? No. He answered his thoughts aloud. The basket of water was sucked upwards into the patch, which became wood again. His hand grew an arm and attached itself to his shoulder. He swallowed. Any trace of copper was gone. Whatever he was looking at had turned dark; whatever he was thinking had slipped his mind. If he could see himself he would see a boy lying on his side with his thumb in his mouth, fast asleep.

Wheels's mother had only to touch him and he sprang to his feet for his early-morning practice. By the time he returned, the whole house was awake. Everyone did something to contribute to Wheels's effort. Red Head and Bash Man Goady fetched water from the standpipe for him to shower with after his morning training session and for their own wash before going to school. They walked to the standpipe together but once they'd filled their buckets they raced home so fast anyone trying to keep up would have had to trot.

There existed, in the minds of those living in Ariel, guidelines which governed how fresh water was to be transported in a receptacle. Red Head and Bash Man Goady had to have containers that matched their sizes. They knew it was no good saying they could carry it when it was empty. They had to imagine it full. Then they would join the queue at the standpipe and when their turn came they'd rinse the bucket to shift any ants or centipedes before filling it to the rim. Bash Man Goady, as a right-hander, would stand on the right side of the bucket and use his left hand to carry it. The left-handed Red Head always stood on the left and used his right hand to carry and his left hand to speed himself up and keep his balance. Both knees would be bent slightly to prevent any bobbing about during the laden-down walk-race back to the house. To know how well they'd done they'd retrace their steps for some of the way and check their trail before Ariel's over-zealous sun obliterated all trace of a spillage. They never fetched water at night when the moon was full, since it was impossible to guarantee they would not spill a single drop. A bucket loaded with water doubles the moon. The reflected moon hates being spilled so much it steps out of the bucket in anger and chases the water-bearer. (Only Sabbatic can fetch water under a full moon. First, his bucket always has at least one hole. The moon gets spilled at the outset so it cannot be surprised by any accidents. Second, he sings throughout in a drawl the moon finds amusing. Third, he walks in a drunken zigzag which the sober find dizzying.) If that moon catches the water-bearer it dashes him up to the sky and the real moon catches him and pastes him to itself where he remains for ever and can be discerned as a stain or shadow on its watery surface.

A radio announcement issued a challenge to Ariel and the surrounding villages to find a wrestler among them who would be willing to fight Singh. So far he'd wrestled the forty miles between Ariel and the capital, slamming opponents on the makeshift canvas rings so hard they'd lost their fillings, breath and bladder contents and capitulated. Army and police champions (there wasn't an air force) represented the government. Each stood against Singh and was dismissed in a variety of head, arm and leg locks that made them resemble figures of eight and different letters of the alphabet. What was expected to be Singh's biggest challenge – a six-hundred-pound German wrestler who followed the road gang with his beer tent – turned out to be a warm-up for him. Gerhard the German had picked up Singh like a twig and hurled him out of the ring. Singh did a controlled landing on his toes and bounced back into the ring over the top ropes. What happened next was barely followed by those at ringside. Apparently Singh sprinted around the beer maker several times, causing his head to spin, then he arranged the confused man's legs in a full lotus with his arms trapped between them and spun him on his back on the canvas.

The crowd at Ariel's rum shop was dumbstruck. They scratched their heads and groins. If the capital couldn't find someone to beat Singh, how could Ariel? Someone suggested old Sabbatic. This raised a laugh. Another volunteered in a disdainful tone that by the time Sabbatic got from his house to the ring the night would be over. More laughs. Sabbatic always walked ten steps forward, four steps back, with a long pause in the middle. He never turned his head. The children pelted sand stones at him whenever he was on the road but from such a safe distance the clumps of red sand would explode a few yards away from him. They taunted him. He must know the earth is round, and if he didn't walk backwards every time he walked forwards, he might fall off.

Red Head's grandfather virtually lived at the rum shop when he was not on business in the capital. He'd return to the house late at night singing in Portuguese. When he got drunk in the afternoons, his unbuttoned shirt exposed a large red V on his chest. His long neck and face were also red. He could have passed for a large, mobile bottle of red rum. If one of the children didn't sidle in their usual wide arc around him, he'd grab the child and shout, 'You're under arrest!', quickly pressing a coin into the child's palm and squeezing it shut.

Sometimes he took Red Head to the rum shop with him as part of his strategy to get his grandson ready for the Draughts Championships the government had organised. Red Head would play draughts against any and every willing adult with the stipulation that they buy him a bottle of ginger beer if they lost. None of the men could beat him. They said the axe had improved his game. He'd take home a dozen or more bottles which he'd distribute to his brother and cousins, uncles and aunts.

He was with his grandfather in the rum shop on the afternoon of the announcement of Singh's search for an opponent. Soon the talk switched from ridiculing Sabbatic. 'Singh going to swing through here without even stopping' and 'If the man belch or fart when he pass, he going flatten we houses.' They stared down the necks of their beer bottles or shook their heads. Red Head was wondering if his grandfather would speak. What Red Head heard caused him such a fright he scattered the pieces of draughts to the floor.

'My son can lay Singh flat out.'

At first, 'Did I just hear him right?' looks were exchanged. Then a collective laugh exploded in the rum shop. Unlike an explosion, this seemed as if it would never subside. Different men in the bar queued up to repeat, between doubling up and much thigh-slapping, one part or another of the old man's statement. 'His son!' 'Lay Singh!' 'Flat out!' Red Head's grandfather examined the nails of his right hand by curling his fingers into his palm then uncurling them as he flipped the back of his hand up. He did this several times and sighed. Both his eyebrows were raised. Every two seconds he leaned his head a little from side to side to improve his perspective.

The thunderous laughter quietened into the odd titter, then smiles, and was soon replaced with inquisitive looks that begged the old man for clarification. Grandad stood up, straightened his back, leaned forwards on the tips of his toes and back onto his heels, took a deep breath and invited anyone in the room to meet his son Bounce in an elimination bout to determine who should face Singh. He said this with his eyes on the door. He was on the tips of his toes at the end of his statement. He had merely to lean forwards by another fraction to propel himself out of the rum shop. There wasn't a trace of anger in his voice but everyone knew he was furious by his use of correct English. He leaned back on his heels, stood still and looked around the smoky room. Red Head smiled and collected up his draughts. A few of the men helped by fishing for the pieces around their feet. A murmur brewed and distributed itself among the smoke fumes. Red Head stepped from the shop's cool shadows into the whitewashed wall of the early afternoon sun hand in hand with his grandfather. Before the two were out of earshot, a remark about Singh having a new victim to tie into a reef knot triggered new guffaws.

'Rain soon fall, let we walk-race.'

Red Head looked but the sky was clear. He shrugged and rose to his grandfather's challenge.

Three trucks of noisy government supporters passed by. They made music by beating tin cans together, hitting the sides of the trucks, whistling and chanting slogans about the People's Party. Red Head tried to shield his eyes and watch. Fists were waved at Grandad. He held up both his fists and shook them defiantly. The fourth truck slowed down and Red Head saw a man take aim with a bucket and shower Grandad. There was whistling, laughter and applause from the truck. Red Head recognised Raj's smell but it was stronger. When he saw the excrement he stopped in his tracks and covered his mouth. Then he grabbed a few sand stones and pelted them but the truck was a long way off by then, though the knocking of cans and the whistles were clear and the dust still bothered his eyes. Grandad told him to stop crying, that he was fine and there was nothing wrong with him that a little soap and water couldn't fix.

At the house he showered and told his story several times. He said he had more important things on his mind than to take on a few imbeciles on the side of the government whose thinking was only skin-deep. 'What do they know about Africa or India? Anyway I'm from Madeira if they want to be exact. Where's Bounce?' he called. 'I want Bounce.'

Grandad and Red Head searched for Bounce in the twelve rooms of the house. His grandfather shouted his name again. The call was taken up first by one person, then by another and another, until everyone joined in the hunt, looking in all the dark corners they knew. They searched wardrobes, under beds, in cupboards and behind chairs. The hunt progressed to the sheds and pens in the back yard. They gave up calling his name. Each knew that Bounce's migraines were sometimes so severe he was unable to speak or bear sunlight and often vomited. They combed the barn where the cart was parked. The harness and reins and halter for the donkey displayed on nails or slung over planks of wood chimed when they were struck. Bags of paddy gave off a musty smell of earth and grass. A fine dust shaken from the dried husks of coconuts hung like particles of oxygen somehow made transparent by the barn's stored atmosphere. A cockerel, isolated from the hens it treaded until they died from exhaustion, with a black pouch over its head (because in addition to its concupiscence it crowed during full moons, woke everyone in the neighbourhood and fooled them into dressing for work at 2.45 a.m.), heard footsteps approach and charged at them with its wings spread and its head lowered. The rope that tethered one of its claws ran out and jerked it back. Deep in the barn the footsteps came to a room that was completely lightproof. Wiry brushes hung on nails, covering every space. They ranged from a hardness that could scrub flesh off a bone to so soft they were used to brush a baby's head. If the children did something exceptionally bad, they were locked in there. Once proved enough to correct them for the rest of their days. The room was not only pitch black, it was cold and soundproofed by the thick brushes. If a child screamed in there his voice amplified and echoed.

When Grandad opened the door, Red Head's grip on his hand tightened and he shuddered. The fine hairs on his body stood up. Twice he swallowed on a lump in his throat. The poor light in the barn crawled into the blackened room of brushes and got less than two feet in the door before it withered and disappeared. Red Head blinked as if he had opened his eyes underwater in a pond dug in the floor of this shrouded place. He reached out with his left hand to the side and felt a tuft of hair that he took for a particularly soft, short-haired brush. He allowed his hand to wander over it and found the surface to be too flat and wide for a brush. The way it ended in a blunt point confirmed it could only belong to one soul in Ariel. He released his grandfather's hand and put his arm around his uncle, who was crouched hugging his knees and rocking slightly. His grandfather kissed the massive proboscidiform, took a black cloth that had to be two yards long to get around it and blindfolded the eyes, then he led his youngest child out of the dark and the barn.

Rain began to fall though the sun was still out. Everyone dashed for shelter. Red Head took Bounce's other hand. The three walked very slowly from the barn to the house in the sunlight and the rain. Red Head looked at his grandfather, who was speaking to Bounce. Fat raindrops hit the buildings and the ground and obscured Grandad's words. Red Head watched the lips, close to Bounce's ear, part and close. The grimace on Bounce's face transformed into a blank expression, then blossomed into a smile. Bounce stopped, freed his hands from his two guides, tore off his blindfold and flung it in the air with a long, loud laugh to the astonishment of everyone except his father. Then he turned and ran, hopped, skipped and jumped, towards the coconut groves as he tore off his shirt and trousers. Red Head followed him, kicked off his trousers and pulled his shirt over his head. His brother sprinted from the house with a loud 'Yahoo!', followed by cousins, nephews, aunts and uncles, all of whom stripped and sprinted after Bounce, bellowing yeehaas and yahoos in a downpour silvered by the sun.

Winged Feet

BOUNCE DISAPPEARED TO the rice fields with the single instruction from Grandad to work without taking his eyes off a point two feet in front of him, whatever his manoeuvres. To Wheels he said, 'Pace is the key to victory.' Wheels walked to the track cleared behind the house with his Racer on his shoulder and began his training laps, which filled the air with whirling dust clouds and the smell of burning tyres, and caused condors floating overhead to fall dizzily to earth.

Bash Man Goady and a few of the other children were out early to catch the sun. They made mudballs for their slingshots. They'd mix clay and water into a thick paste, break off small clumps and roll them between their palms into balls. These were placed in neat rows on the corrugated zinc roof of a shed to bake in the sun. During the two-hour wait they'd sit in the shade within sight of the roof and argue over who would be the best shot and about past exploits, occasionally loading air into the tongues of their slingshots, taking aim at an invisible target and releasing it with a thwack. At last they'd collect their ammunition off the roasting roof and distribute it. Then, their pockets filled, they'd load their slingshots with a mud pellet and head for the bushes to hunt small birds. After several wild shots someone would get lucky and stun a bird. It would flap around dazed until a heavy rock was brought down on its head. The oldest in the group would pick off the feathers, clean out the insides and cut off the head. A makeshift fire was kindled with much fanning and blowing on a few sticks and dry leaves. The bird was roasted on the end of a stick the children would each take a turn holding and revolving over the flames, then divided equally among them and devoured. Even the bones were chewed to powder and swallowed.

Granny was hanging washing on the clothesline or taking it off or both. Red Head couldn't be sure. She rose so early it was conceivable that she had already completed one wash and was merely clearing the line to make room for another. From the regular squelch, squelch, squelch that poured into his ears, Red Head tried to picture one of his aunts bunched over a scrubbing board murdering one garment after another. He hoped it was his loving aunt Footsy of the articulate feet and water-bearing thighs.

'I said, your move.'

'Sorry, I was miles away.'

Red Head pushed his first draught forwards in time to crush a red ant crossing a white square on the chequered board.

'I hope you will think of better reasons than that for moving a piece when it comes to the actual championships.'

'Sorry, Grandad.' He sat upright as taught by his schoolteacher. A clean-shaven Monday-morning face popped into his head. Teacher, as he was known to the class, began the week with a smooth, hairless face and by Wednesday afternoon he'd be sporting a full beard. He wore his shirt sleeves rolled up. When his arms were touched they felt downy as a duck-feather pillow. The children believed his entire body was covered with hairs as long and thick as feathers. Raj said the feathers on Teacher's body were there because he came from northern India where the nights were cold and the early mornings were misty and damp. Raj held up his arm and said his bald limb was from the south. The boys would deliberately try and touch Teacher's bare arms before the school day ended but the girls would run home if he accidentally brushed against them.

'Your move. What's the matter with you today?'

Red Head shrugged his shoulders.

'Answer your grandad.'

'There will be red, then there will be black.'

'Let your grandad tell you something his grandad told him.'

A shout came from the field at the back of the house. Bash Man Goady and the other children sprinted towards it. Red Head walk-raced his grandfather. Sand raised by Wheels had funnelled up over the roof of the house and the trees and formed a floating mountain whose peak penetrated the sky. But the sand at the base of the mountain had suddenly stopped and cleared. All that red earth was simply drifting away by the time Red Head and Grandad reached the field. Wheels, Red Head thought, who had made that mountain, must have cycled up it all the way to paradise, and he had pulled up its moorings behind him so that he could not be followed or brought back to ordinary ground.

Red Head and his grandfather were the last to get there. Wheels was on his feet with Beanstalk attending to the bicycle. Bash Man Goady and the other children ringed them. 'Blasted bird, it dived right at me! Now look at my front wheel.' But everyone was looking at his left leg. Wheels stopped remonstrating and gesticulating at the dead condor and his damaged bicycle and followed everyone's eyes to his leg. His left side, from his hip down to his ankle, had no skin; it had ripped off as he slid to a stop on the track. Everyone stared at the reddening flesh. A single, black condor feather fringed with white protruded from his lower calf.

'Winged feet,' Red Head whispered.

Grandad pulled the feather out of his son and sank it out of sight in his shirt pocket. 'Carry your brother to the house.'

Beanstalk lifted Wheels by his right side. His raw left side was held high in the light. A bright red dripped off him and darkened in the dull red sand.

The children stared. 'Will he live?' one of them enquired.

Grandad laughed, 'Of course, don't worry,' and ruffled a few heads within reach. To distract them he asked who would like to help him carry the bicycle back to the house. All the children made sure they got at least one hand to grip the bicycle they were never allowed to touch.

'Wings,' someone whispered and they all mouthed 'wings' in agreement, with hands outstretched to the racing bike.

Red Head spent the late afternoon with his girlfriend Sten, the youngest of six sisters who lived two fields away. They picked downs from a tree. He climbed the tree and used his weight to shake a branch. She sheltered her head from the hail and shrieked. She was busy loading downs into the front of her dress held up with one hand by the time he'd climbed down to the lowest branch, swung from it and dropped to his feet. She held her dress with both hands to make more room while he gathered the marble-sized fruit and piled them there. Then they built a house by leaning a few dead coconut branches against the downs tree, eating as they worked, spitting the downs seeds at each other and keeping score of the hits. A few of the branches were adjusted after the two stood back and examined their house. They crawled into it and closed the gap behind them. A handful of rice was cooked in a tin of boiling water balanced on stones surrounding a little fire they had to blow on to keep alive. When the rice was ready – both tasted it to make sure – they killed the fire with handfuls of sand. The tin pot doubled as a plate. Using two bits of husk shaved from a green coconut, they took turns to spoon out the rice and occasionally fed each other.

They belched and laughed and tried to belch some more but felt sick so stopped. Then Red Head plaited Sten's long shiny black hair into a clumsy rope that fell to the small of her back as she sang a string of popular Hindi songs. As soon as he was finished she lay down and he lay beside her and they watched the afternoon light stealing between the braids of the coconut branches and striping their bodies.

'You look like a red zebra.'

'You look like a black zebra.'

'Zebras are black and white.'

'Then how can I be a red zebra?'

'Your red skin in these bars of light.'

'And your black skin in it too.'

'Our children will be red and black zebras.'

'What a nice mix-up.'

Sten hummed a little or else Red Head hummed. Sten heard her sister calling her across two fields. Red Head looked at her and they smiled and listened to her name getting near. She did not move, not until she'd judged by the increasing loudness of her sister's shout of 'Sten, Sten, Sten', which lacked any trace of urgency or annoyance, that she had passed through the side gate and entered the back yard.

That night the sky over Ariel resembled a barn stocked with a delicate crop of cloud. A full moon played hide-and-seek with itself, dashing behind them, then stepping clear in an exuberant blaze. If it could be seen, the wind that pitchforked the gigantic bales in the barn from one end of Ariel to another would be fantastically muscled. It flung Sabbatic's discordant singing to the children's ear too loud and too clear for them to believe anything other than that he was standing in the yard below their bedrooms. It interspersed Sabbatic's wailing with a long howling complaint from the tall coconut groves. Dried coconuts crashed to the ground as if the trees cried hardened tears. The mule kicked its pen, blaming it for the commotion. Then the door of the giant barn was swung open on its hinges by the wind and banged one, two, three, four, five times, and the banging and Sabbatic's crooning and the howling coconuts were all supplanted by screams.

Red Head opened his eyes and listened. What had made the sound of a scream? Not Sabbatic. Not the wind in the trees. Not pigs, that was a squeal. Not dogs. Not the mule, those were brays. He thought of Sten when he shook the branch of the downs tree and she made a noise close to a scream. The house continued to doze, rocked by the wind. Red Head sat upright, made alert and edgy by it. He panicked. 'Gunfire! Screams from Sten's house!'

He left the bedroom he shared with Bash Man Goady and three other cousins to find his uncles and aunts and Granny gathered in the living room. They looked at him with the sleep of the house in their eyes, unsure whether to reprimand or congratulate him as they waited to register for themselves the high chorus above the coconut trees, above the braying mule, the squeals from the pigpen and the new addition of the cock that had been cured of its haphazard crowing, now in a state of complete relapse.

The door in the sky banged twice. This time the screams found a pitch higher than Sabbatic and all the animals and trees. Recognition flicked the sleep from everyone's face and made the uncles jump for lamps and cutlasses and dive into the night. Red Head looked at his aunt Footsy and cried. She hugged him. Other children joined in with Red Head's crying. Bash Man Goady punched the wall. He made a few steps towards the door where his uncles had disappeared but Granny touched his arm. He struck the wall again and fumed. Granny pulled him to her and hugged him and he took that as his signal to cry.

The children squeezed into every available window space to follow the progress of the lamps across the fields to Sten's house. But the lamps were blown out in the open and the moon was nowhere in sight. Screams continued from Sten's house, renewing the crying among the children. Red Head felt giddy. He sat on the floor and swallowed on a taste of copper. Footsy knelt beside him and peered into his face. The screams abated. Again, the animals and trees and Sabbatic took up their shared inheritance. The door banged once, twice. So near, the roof of the barn must have lowered and the barn door tilted towards the children and slammed a third time. Aunts screamed and pulled the children to the floor. Parts of the house splintered. Granny began to pray. 'Merciful God. Spare the children from the work of the devil. They haven't had their lives. Take me in their place, God.' The children screamed, terrified by Granny's prayer.

Red Head fell into his aunt's arms and she eased him to the floor. He stiffened, stretched his limbs and shuddered. His eyes rolled in his head. He gritted his teeth and saliva rolled down his cheek. Footsy cradled his head in her hands and Granny pushed away the chair Red Head had kicked. The children stopped crying and stared. Bash Man Goady cried and tried to help but Granny told him there was nothing to do but make sure his brother did not hurt himself on the furniture and that he got air. Bash Man Goady took this to mean his brother should have space to breathe, so he ordered the other children to step back. As he held out his arms and pushed them, he glanced over his shoulder at Red Head twitching on the floor. He wished his mother or father were there even though he knew there was no better nurse than Granny for his brother. He blinked rapidly to clear the water in his eyes but his nose ran so he gave up herding his nephews and cousins back and wiped his nose on his sleeves and watched his brother's twitches lessen and a calm settle on his face.

Wheels and Beanstalk banged on the back door and shouted to be let in. Granny unbolted the bottom half of the door and they ducked into the house. They said they'd left Bounce to guard the sisters and returned when they heard shots and screams coming from here. Grandad's voice interrupted their report. He came up the drive shouting the names of his children, their wives and his grandchildren. He was accompanied by the entire population of the rum shop, all of whom had sobered up the instant they heard the gunfire.

'They shouted "coolie lover".' Beanstalk's words silenced the crowd in the yard.

Grandad held a gas lamp high in front of him. Its glow fell like the flaps of a tent about them, shutting out the dark night. As Grandad began to speak, a strong moon emerged from a bundle of clouds and cast shadows as hard as flesh and bone. Everyone shone under that moon. The demarcations of white, brown and black that were so apparent in daylight were softened by the moon to subtle gradations of tone. If people were intent on locating such differences they would have to look hard and long in this equalising light. They would have to strain their eyes and get so close to the subject their noses would virtually connect with the skin under scrutiny. Grandad spoke of men who'd married women they'd fallen in love with regardless of race and who had themselves been the products of various unions between the races. He pointed to the fact that he was Portuguese, his wife African, one daughter-in-law half Amerindian, another Indian. Let them try and separate us. Let them try.

Everyone applauded Grandad and shook hands. They divided into groups of five or so and headed in all directions, intent on apprehending the perpetrators.

Red Head was unsteady on his feet. He walked up to Beanstalk, who assured him that Sten and her family were all unhurt and safe. He wanted to see Sten for himself but Footsy steered him in the direction of the bedroom and told him he had seen enough excitement for one night.

The mule was returned to its pen. A bucket of slop was poured in the pig trough, which had the immediate effect of silencing their squeals for the squelch of them snorkling it. An aunt threw some seed at the cockerel to entice it to peck instead of crow.

Red Head overheard Grandad asking Granny what kind of madness had happened tonight. He strained his ears for her reply but found he was listening to his own rapid heart and breath. His lips mouthed the words uttered by a small voice in his head: There was red, then there was black. He understood that the red was not the sand road but blood and the black was not the new, smooth covering on the road but skin, black and brown skin and red for blood. He would have to explain to his grandfather but he could not raise his heavy head off the pillow. His body felt light and unable to move, afloat and moored to his bedding on the floor. If he had the winged feet of Wheels he would fly from here with Sten and her sisters, his brother, aunts, grandmother, grandfather, uncles, cousins and nephews, even old Sabbatic, if he could silence his singing, and Miss Metage and that confused cockerel, confined and in its black headgear once more.

Growee and Alligator

'GROWEE!' CAME THE shout in the miles-long coconut grove as Bash Man Goady spotted the young coconut plant. Uncles, aunts and cousins combing the grove spread in a line twenty yards apart, broke rank and rushed to the find where Bash Man Goady pointed at the plant as if his index finger had zapped it into being. Beanstalk pulled the plant clear of the ground, shook off the red dirt, stripped away the young shoots with his cutlass, then split the bark for the honeyed growth inside. He motioned with his cutlass for Red Head to approach him. Balancing a handful of growee on the tip of the cutlass, he held it steady. Red Head prised off the milky flesh.

'Is the brains this, you know, the brains and heart of the coconut tree and Miss Metage say is the only thing that can cure my head.' The others nodded in agreement with Red Head and from the looks on their faces it was clear that they too wished they'd been chopped on the forehead by an axe. Beanstalk gave everyone a taste of what was left and Bounce wrapped a small portion saved for the recuperating Wheels in a dasheen leaf and placed it in his pocket. The milky juice peeped out of the corners of Red Head's mouth as he chewed. He shot out his tongue and swiped his lips clean. Then they spread themselves into a line again.

These growee hunts had increased not only to procure Miss Metage's prescription for Red Head but as a substitute for the shortgage of guavas that had hit the countryside. The once ubiquitous fruit, which children had used as squashy missiles when overripe to plaster each other in guava-wars, were now as rare as Blue Mountain coffee beans. They blamed the Chinese retailer who innocently sold the first bottle of guava extract as a rare perfume. Men who caught the merest whiff of this aroma on the nape of a woman's neck both watered at the mouth like toothless infants and exhibited the more adult passion of crying inconsolably for the attentions of that woman until their shirt fronts became stuck to their bodies and stained with drool and tears. When their tears and saliva ran out they cried with dried eyes and wide, dry mouths and sounded like tractor engines turning over. When their voices abandoned them, their eyes and mouths performed the antics of crying as expressed by the giants of silent movies. Men afflicted with the ailment of having sniffed the new perfume bore the one trademark: whether starched or wrinkled, their shirts retained the same badge of bitter spit and tears.

Soon these men were intolerable to others who'd refused to enter into the same trance of lovesickness. They were assiduously avoided and therefore drank in the same rum shops customised to meet their idiosyncratic diet of guava: guava jelly, spread lovingly on guava bread, for breakfast; lunch comprised guava in a red pepper and thyme mix, baked in a flour base, with more guavas for pudding, the pink-fleshed, seed-infested centres hollowed out and spiced with cinnamon or ginger and sweetened with raisins or honey, then refilled and baked in clay ovens; for afternoon tea, guava cake, washed down by a condiment, in which milk curdled, made by adding water at 99 degrees centigrade to dried guava seeds; at night they drank the overproof pink liquid fermented in vats of trodden guavas and ate the skins of guavas or chewed dried guava seeds.

The stomachs of guava lovers ballooned. People misread this, claiming that the love was blessed since it made men fat while other men, equally in love but not influenced by guava, remained rakes or dumplings as they had begun. This presumption held for one month after the theory was propounded. A guava lover discredited it. On the thirty-first day he walked into the bright afternoon in a drunken zigzag and fell under a truck supplying the road gang. His bloated mass wedged against the chassis and dragged along the newly paved road. People who thought the trail was part of the truck's shed payload corrected themselves when upon closer examination they could see that it ended where the body lay and consisted of millions of guava seeds. The coroner's report concluded that the body had ceased being dragged along the road at the point that it did, because a sizeable portion of guava bound up in it had been lost through six of the body's seven openings, thereby enabling it to become thin enough to slide from under the chassis. The truck sounded its melodic horn throughout the three hundred and sixty-five yard ordeal, but failed to stop.

'Growee' was what everyone wanted to hear but Beanstalk yelled, 'Trench!', bringing the hunt in the coconut grove to a standstill. Up to now the expedition had done brilliantly with discovery after discovery of a young coconut shoot punctuating the meticulous forward search at regular intervals. Faced with the trench the long line dissolved. Everyone to Beanstalk's left and right congregated around him. Beanstalk led the assembly on a twisting path next to the trench in search of its narrowest point, where, ideally, everyone would cross without getting wet.

Bash Man Goady began the rhyme game. 'Growee is good, growee is sweet, growee knocks me off my feet.'

Everyone repeated it. The duty of the person who started the game was to select someone who should continue it, either by calling their name at the end of the rhyme or by pointing at them. Bash Man Goady cocked the hammer of his thumb, stretched his index and middle finger into barrels in his brother's direction and fired noiselessly. Red Head grabbed the area around his heart, staggering like a miniature Rudolph Valentino, to buy time as his mind reeled to compose something. 'Growee for breakfast, growee for dinner, don't fast, eat growee and be a winner.'

Everyone cheered and repeated it. They watched him edgily, not wanting to be next, yet knowing the longer it took to be chosen in one of these rhyme games, the harder the task of composition as the options lessened. Red Head lobbed a grenade at Bounce by bowling overarm. Bounce had his eyes on the trench and didn't see. Everyone shouted, 'Bounce!' He leapt back several feet from the trench. Bounce's fright made them double up hysterically. The search in the shaded grove came to a complete stop. Just as someone recovered his composure he'd look at Bounce or someone else and that would start him laughing again.

'Over here.' Beanstalk had gone a little way ahead. By the time they caught up with him, he was already making his way down the steep bank of the trench. He had chosen a point where several dead coconut branches had fallen and obscured the water, partly covering a fat log situated perfectly across it.

The children would need assistance to get down the bank. Footsy and Bounce positioned themselves a few feet apart with the intention of passing the children from one to the other down the bank.

Beanstalk stepped once, twice, then a third time on the log, which shifted to the left, then to the right, shaking off the branches and the mud and stirring the stagnant trench. The swift movement lasted about two seconds, yet it caught everyone's attention. They saw Beanstalk's fight to keep his balance. He threw his arms out to his sides and adjusted his body in two jagged movements, one to the left, another to the right. They saw how the camouflage of mud and branches was discarded to reveal the six-foot-long, mottled

53

back and tapered tail of an alligator, whose head reared and whose massive jaws separated to show a wide, startlingly white cavern. They were too busy cycling through the air to mount a tree, any tree, or running in a zigzag as instructed to do if pursued by an alligator, to see Beanstalk jump high above the alligator, so high, in fact, that he seemed to be treading the air like a hummingbird. At that precise point in the air he removed a rope collected around his shoulder and opened a loop at one end. As he descended he held the loop in one hand and the end of the rope in the other. When he was about to land where a log was presumed to be but now an alligator's jaws snapped, he drew up his knees, passed the loop under his feet and encircled the jaws. He tightened the loop and snapped the jaws shut as he obeyed the laws of gravity and splashed into the trench. The tail whipped at him. Beanstalk skipped over it. It lashed at him again. This time he lassoed it to the other end of the rope. He struggled to hold the rope and prevent the alligator from swinging at him again. One blow to the legs and he knew his bones would break. As Bounce spun round from his retreat and flung himself down the bank, Beanstalk grabbed the tail. It swung and flung him several feet away. He fell on his back in the trench. The alligator's jaws were clamped but it dashed towards him. Beanstalk dug his heels into the mud and grasped at the weeds thriving in it as he attempted to back away. His eyes widened and his mouth opened as the alligator closed the gap between them. The rope around the jaws loosened and the alligator paused and shook it off. Its jaws opened. Beanstalk stared into the white cave and squeezed his lids together in preference to the darkness behind them. Bounce dropped onto one knee between the feet of his brother, barely an arm's length from the alligator, which ran into a tremendous butt from Bounce's prodigious head. The alligator bounded back and Bounce fell between his brother's legs. Then the reptile straightened on its four piano legs and toppled over, stunned.

Beanstalk and Bounce scrambled upright and lassoed the mouth together. They strapped its head and tail to a pole and carried it from the trench. The eyelids of the alligator flicked open; it wriggled uselessly and frothed at the mouth. Suddenly it went quite still as if resigned to its new condition as a captive.

'He got bubbles on his back.' Red Head began a rhyme as they marched back to the house. 'Alligator one, alligator two, alligator snapped at Beanstalk shoe.'

Everyone repeated it as Red Head pulled a pin with his teeth from an imaginary grenade and bowled to Footsy. She added, 'Alligator three, alligator four, alligator still like a log on the floor.' As they repeated it, Footsy hopped on her right leg and pointed at Bounce with a twig which she'd swept up between the toes of her left foot.

Bounce glanced at the alligator he and Beanstalk shouldered and began, 'Alligator five, alligator six, walking in the air strapped to a stick.' They clapped and whistled.

'Bubble Back!' Red Head shouted. Index fingers whipped against the clasped middle fingers and thumbs. The alligator bobbed up and down to the brothers' walking rhythm. It was so still it appeared attentive, as though listening for the next instalment of the rhyme about it. Two big, black, unwinking eyes reflected a spherical coconut grove peopled with little skipping, convex figures.

Hassau and Alligator

THE UNCLES KEPT Bubble Back on a fat rope tied around a guava tree devoid of fruit; a rope long enough for him to crawl from the paltry shade offered by the tree into the shell pond. Bubble Back's favourite pose was to face the house in a lazy guard duty for children with his head resting on the bank and his body submerged in the clear water. When the children came to watch him he would take a deep breath, slide from the bank and disappear to the remotest part of the pond, using up all the slack in his lead.

Mostly, he was ignored, except at dusk when it was showtime for Bubble Back. The uncles would drag him out of the pond to allow the children to swim and set him loose in a fenced field where he became their mad bull. At first he would ignore the prods from the uncles' sticks and the shouts from those ranged along the top of the fence, then he would suddenly get mad, raise his belly off the ground and charge them on his four piano legs. The uncles would demonstrate the art of running in a zigzag to escape an alligator, jumping onto the fence in plenty of time to avoid Bubble Back's snapping jaws. To get him back on his leash, Beanstalk would tease Bubble Back with a rope. As Bubble Back charged at him, Beanstalk would float over the alligator with his incapacitating lasso. Then they would drag Bubble Back from the field and secure the rope to the unfecund guava tree for the night.

Bubble Back seemed to grow fat. Everyone put this down to the luxury of captivity: set meals; a home he didn't have to defend; insufficient exercise in the little fenced field. And, as if in response to their discussions, he grew thin overnight so they thought nothing further of it. When the children complained about missing the shell pond at times of the day other than the allotted swim at dusk, Bounce and Beanstalk decided to drag Bubble Back to the field. Bubble Back dug his feet into the ground and tried to snap chunks out of the uncles. He swung his tail in an effort to break their legs. Bounce and Beanstalk couldn't understand why Bubble Back was making all this fuss. Bounce seriously considered butting him into submission. The children watched, a little puzzled. Once Bubble Back was dragged clear of the area, they dived into the shell pond. They decided to play 'catcher'. The first person to do the catching was chosen by a rhyme which Red Head sang as he pointed to each person.

> 'Apten dapten dee calapten
> Daddy calapten dee do
> Eskamo dee scalamascoo dee
> Apten dapten dee calapten
> Daddy calapten dee do.'

He finished it as he pointed to himself so he had to be the catcher. Everyone scattered from him, splashing water as they kicked and paddled to get away. Whoever he touched first would have to take over the chase. He considered going after Bash Man Goady but changed his mind since he didn't want to be accused by his brother of picking on him just because they were brothers.

They all took the dark shadow swimming around their feet for a bird flying overhead. Not just circling on one wingbeat every now and again like carrion crows, but flying as if in an aerial display that involved rolls, spins, about-turns, dives and swivels. The bird surfaced for air and, instead of a beak and feathers, the children were greeted by a much scaled-down version of Bubble Back, its mouth agape. The pond became a trampoline all the children had landed on together: they flew out of it with the velocity at which they'd dived in, decorated with screams.

Grandad decreed that Bubble Back was a she. Mother and baby were reunited. After the elections they'd be returned to the coconut grove. All the children groaned with disappointment. They said they wished the elections could be postponed for ever, then Bubble Back could stay for ever. The teasing in the field ceased. Bash Man Goady suggested that they should call the baby Double Back because it was an exact miniature replica of its mother. Red Head wondered how long a baby alligator could live away from its mother. He wanted to be Double Back. He didn't care if his life as an alligator would be miserable compared to his life now. Next to his mother he would be a happy little alligator. He wouldn't notice the rope around his neck and the limited amount of slack that would be a constant reminder of his station at the guava tree. He would be next to his mother. Yes, Double Back was the luckiest creature in the world.

If the children weren't at school they'd play, pick fruit or go fishing. They liked to catch hassau, the sweetest of fishes. A child can catch them barehanded during their nesting season. The females lay their eggs near the top of the water and whisk the surface with their tails to notify the males of the location of the eggs. The males telegraph their readiness to fertilise any eggs that care for their sperm by also beating the face of the trench with their tails.

The children compelled hassau to the surface by wriggling their wrists in the water. Hassau floated into their hands mesmerised by the promise of playing a major role in the procreation chain, despite the fact that it involved no touching. Red Head was entranced by this activity alone – lying on his stomach at the edge of the trench, making bubbles froth around his hand, throwing the fishes over his shoulder to the ground where they danced until exhausted and covered in red sand – when he noticed one of the bigger bubbles acted as a couch for Half Pint, who had his legs crossed, his arms folded and a foolish, broad grin on his face. Red Head pushed back from the pond. Half Pint curled and uncurled his index finger at Red Head, who edged to the trench lying on his stomach but with his hands drawn back from the water. Half Pint cupped his hands around his mouth and shouted, 'There were four! You don't understand I have a job to do. I won't go until you admit there were four! You know I can be nasty.' His tone was reprimanding and exasperated. 'And I don't mean by just saying it. You have to do something about it.' A hassau surfaced under the bubble Half Pint sat on and burst it. Half Pint toppled into the trench and vanished.

Bash Man Goady approached. 'What you looking for? You gone blind? The fish right under your nose? Grandad looking for you to practise draughts with him.' Bash Man Goady helped him to gather up the fishes on the bank. They walked back to the house in single file.

'Will Daddy ever come back?'

'No. Forget him.'

'He left because of us.'

'No. Is something between Mummy and him.'

'How come Mummy not writing?'

'Why you asking me? I look like the postman?'

The idea that they might have been abandoned rendered the brothers speechless and exhausted. Another word would be a waste of breath. What little energy they had left in them would be sunk into the walk back to the house. Motherless. Perhaps. Fatherless. Definitely. Crickets chirped in the tall razor grass and bounced out of the path of their bare feet. Red Head timed his steps to fall into the track made by his brother. The moment his brother's heel lifted off the ground, the ball of Red Head's forward foot descended in its place. It required such concentration not to bump his brother's heel and cause a fight that the cloud of his mother and three younger brothers, which had darkened his mind, slipped its moorings and drifted away.

He sat opposite his grandad with the draughts board arranged between them. Grandad pinned his nostrils. Red Head told him he had been fishing. Grandad opened the game by moving the draught in the left corner of the front row towards the middle of the board. 'What did you catch?'

Red Head was about to reply when he spotted Half Pint on the draught he intended to move. He leaned back suddenly.

Grandad cast him a quizzical look. 'Come on, is not such a good move.' Red Head's eyes darted from Grandad's face to Half Pint, who began to tap-dance on the draught, and back. Grandad looked at the board and at Red Head, then at the board. 'You see something I don't?'

Half Pint piped up, 'Don't make a fool of yourself, Red Head. He can't see me or hear me.' To prove his point, Half Pint resumed his tap-dance with even more vigour and sang 'Mr Bojangles' at the top of his voice. Red Head squashed Half Pint under his thumb and pushed the draught piece hard into the board.

'Another ant?' Grandad frowned.

Red Head denied it and smiled. His joy vanished when Half Pint materialised on the draught Red Head was contemplating as his next move. Red Head leaned back so far he tipped onto his spine.

'What's the matter with you?' An annoyed Grandad peered at him.

'I sorry, Grandad.' Half Pint jumped clear as Red Head picked up the draught piece, shook it and placed it on the square opposite the first draught his grandad had moved.

'Is not a die.' Grandad pitched him a frown.

Half Pint hurdled three draughts and settled on the one Red Head wanted to move. 'As you may have surmised, my little rusty-headed friend, I can read your thoughts.' Red Head watched Half Pint for any lip movement but the diminutive devil had his left hand covering his mouth while the outstretched right hand described small circles as he bowed his head. 'It therefore follows that we can converse without you having to speak. So get on with it!' Red Head wanted to abandon the game.

According to the children it was helicopter season in Ariel. The single rotary arm of the crisp seeds rode the wind, swivelling soundlessly. Everyone would gather under a tree and, using one hand, try to catch a seed as it glided and rotated to the ground. Half Pint imitated the helicopter motion of the seed by pirouetting a few inches above the draught piece and alighting delicately. Red Head looked at him with menace.

'I am not the one who's wasting time. I want to hear about the fourth image. If you can't play draughts and communicate with me at the same time, just say the word and I'll take over for you.'

Red Head wanted to see this so he nodded in agreement.

'No outward movements please, just think.'

Red Head apologised.

'Forget it,' Half Pint said dismissively, then positioned himself on the bridge of Red Head's nose. He felt a small weight that reminded him of Granny's half-spectacles, which he sometimes tried.

'Stop crossing your eyes and concentrate,' Grandad ordered.

Red Head's next two moves gave away three of his pieces but his third and fourth each won him a pair of Grandad's most promising pieces and positioned him with one move per piece to crown two kings. Grandad sat upright, reached over and rubbed his grandson's head, toppling Half Pint off the boy's nose. Half Pint informed Red Head that he could only win the championships if he 'cooperated'. He straddled Red Head's nose, facing him. Red Head squinted. 'Stop crossing your eyes,' Grandad repeated, a little sterner this time.

A new game began. Red Head thought about the moves after they were made by his hand. His grandfather called Footsy and Granny, who were nearby, as he arranged the pieces for another game. Half Pint nodded in approval as Red Head conjured an image of a kite, allowing it to come into focus and fill his mind while he devoted a small portion of his intelligence to studying the draughts board. Half Pint guided him. He knew which piece to move to counter Grandad before Grandad actually made the move. He saw a kite flying without anyone to control it. The elongated tail of the kite glinted with what Red Head took to be razor blades. Far below the kite's tail a limousine emblazoned with the presidential seal sped along the red sand road that ran from the capital to the interior. When the car turned a corner the kite described the same curve in the sky. When it accelerated along a straight, the kite ascended in a perfect line. As it slowed, the kite descended. Red Head found himself manoeuvring the kite above the limousine and lowering it to the point where the tail touched the roof though the car was speeding along. The razor blades that glinted far in the sky now bunched together and looked nothing like the hazard-ous decoration the children put on the tails of their kites at the end of the kite-flying season to cut each other out of the sky in their serious kite-wars. In their place he saw a bundle attached to the end of the kite's tail. His eyes on the bundle acted like a detonator. An explosion shattered the limousine and its prized contents, not with a bang, this was soundless, but with blackness. All the things that furnished his mind to capacity: the kite, the limousine and its motorcade, the red sand road, the house and the yard, all the surrounding fields, the shell pond and the coconut groves, all vanished into this blackness.

Nooooo! Red Head's shout reverberated around his chest as it searched for an outlet. The small group around him and his grandad applauded another victory. 'He's sweating. Let the child rest,' Granny ordered. Grandad said the dice-shaking stuff and the crossing of the eyes were sound distraction techniques. Footsy swept Red Head up in her arms and kissed him. 'You clever little man! Before you, nobody round here could beat your grandad.' Half Pint flew off his nose. Granny handed him a glass of mauby, which he gulped down.

'You ready for the championships.' Grandad ruffled his head.

Footsy led him into the kitchen. 'I curried your fishes for you.' He had hoped to cook them with Sten but he smiled at his aunt and thanked her. She ladled the hassau curry onto a deep plate and buttered two slices of bread the way Red Head liked to see her do it – by holding the knife in the toes of her right foot. Many little Half Pints ascended in the steam of the curry to the ceiling. All clapped and smiled at Red Head, who attacked the stew with his bread to scatter the steam.

A radio announcer described the scene at the start of the National Cycle Championships: 'Two hundred cyclists lined up in twenty rows of ten.' Wheels was assigned to the fourth row after time trials in which he was beaten on the clock by all thirty-five cyclists from the city, a fact which Grandad disputed with the impassive, government-appointed racing officials until Wheels assured them the whole thing would be resolved by the outcome of the race.

At the 9 a.m. start the sun was high enough to have dried to a crisp any amount of washing put on a clothesline ninety minutes earlier. A fine, unearned sheet of sweat covered all the contestants, officials and bystanders, and the harsh light made them all squint. A spume of red sand floated over the proceedings. An interior minister at the starting line mopped his forehead and neck with a huge white handkerchief, which he folded with care as he spoke to officials and placed into his back pocket, only to retrieve it moments later for another swipe at his forehead and neck.

Wheels visualised the road ahead: its ruts and potholes, its long tracts of sometimes flawless, sometimes treacherous red sand winding from the interior to the capital in twists and about-turns, hairpin bends and straight stretches, and the occasional letter S as the road mimicked a river, following unseen gradients and contours that defined this countryside. He had two bottles of water, one slung over each shoulder and tucked on the shortened straps under each arm. In a tiny fob pocket on his red polyester jersey he had tucked one of Granny's sugar cakes, made with desiccated coconut, for sustenance. Grandad's advice to him was delivered like a sermon. He should save the tidbit for the final stretch into the capital, when all his muscles would feel as if they were being turned on a spit over a blazing fire.

At the starter's gun, fired some sixty miles from Ariel, there was great applause and cheers from everyone at the house grouped around the radio. They knew it would be nearly two hours before the leading pack approached the bend into Ariel. Almost two hours of praying for Wheels's survival and strength and hoping all the attention devoted to Wings would keep it operative and free of mechanical failures at a time when it was being ridden at its hardest on the red sand road. Two of the longest hours during which chores were attempted and abandoned in preference to joining one or other of the little groups waiting in the shade of trees or on verandas, positioning themselves on chairs, on foot, on the ground, so that they could keep the road in their sights and discuss the various probabilities governing a victory for Wheels. Ariel would be put on the map. The house would become a tourist attraction. Wheels would turn into a national hero. That was the plan and nothing stood between it and actual fact except one hundred miles of the country's main road and perhaps thirty-five other cyclists. Where was Wheels now but at the front, leading the pack into each bend and leaning with his inside pedal uppermost, then sprinting out of the saddle, his body thrown forwards, his head lowered and Wings gyrating from left to right under him with each thrust of his legs; head down to avoid the flying sand with his eyes cast a few feet ahead watching for an obstruction. Their talk even placed Wheels some yards in front of the chasing pack and minutes from the bulk of the other riders.

The transistor they were huddled around did not name Wheels as one of the leaders but it was conceivable that he was stuck in the middle of the leading pack and was not identifiable through all the sand. A few of the sprinters from the capital were named among the leaders. This dampened the speculation somewhat and furrowed many brows. Grandad said Wheels knew it was early days in the race to take the strain of the lead for a little short-lived glory, he was too smart for that. Instead, he was safely tucked in the middle of that leading pack biding his time.

The biggest peril to the riders was the tendency of the cars and motorcycles that formed a convoy at the head of the race to fall back too close to them. Sand would be whipped into their faces, forcing them to ride with their eyes closed and trust that the road was clear of potholes. Each time the vehicles drew near, the riders would wave them away frantically and even lessen their pace in order to widen the gap. When two riders touched, one would push the other away, causing him to veer into someone else. But these disturbances rippled quickly through the bunched men, who would settle again into their task with aplomb.

Soon traffic through Ariel was reduced from a trickle to the odd vehicle rushing home to secure a spectator's space by the roadside. Then it dried up altogether and some children ventured out into the middle of the road to do a short twist or to wriggle their bottoms before darting back into yards. The noon light that should have been blinding by now and scalding had softened to a haze. Footsy remarked that the sun had taken pity on the cyclists and was shining at half strength. As they examined the sky they saw not a sun shying away from its natural function but an approaching dust storm flung so far and wide it might have been a net intent on capturing the sun. The storm crept across the sky as they stared and seemed to grow in stature until it loomed overhead. Soundless up to now, Ariel's inhabitants stared at it. They were startled by a sound that emanated from the sandstorm. Red Head craned his neck as if to listen more attentively. Others trailed off in their speech and inclined their heads. Some cupped a hand behind their ear. Red Head thought the sound came from the flat strip of wood saved from an ice lolly into which a small slit was made and a length of string attached before it was spun. This had to be a thousand such sticks spun at once. He looked in the opposite direction of the sandstorm since the sound seemed to bounce off the sky, which had become curved like a drum, elastic and resonant.

Bash Man Goady jumped and shouted, 'They coming! They coming!'

Vehicles mounted with bicycles, police cars and motorcycles with flashing lights rounded the bend into Ariel, gesturing madly to everyone to stay clear of the road. When the clouds of sand raised by these vehicles had thinned, everyone could see the bend gaping empty and hungry for occupancy. Suddenly five men, perhaps six, materialised on bright red, yellow, green and blue racing bikes which they leaned on precariously into the corner, hugging it. They sprang off their saddles in unison and sprinted into the straight. A crunching and whistling could be discerned above the cheers and applause of the crowd lining the road. And there, matching the men surrounding him gesture for gesture, revolution by revolution of his bicycle wheels, was none other than Wheels on Wings. A roar of recognition rose from Ariel's population as everyone hugged, leapt into the air and screamed his name.

As planned, Wheels worked his way into the front of the group, then veered to the left side of the road as he approached the house. Two fresh bottles of water, one held by Bounce and fifty yards later the other by Beanstalk, were grabbed by Wheels, who even managed a smile. Seconds earlier he had dumped the empty ones at the feet of the children, who scrambled and fought each other to possess either of these valued trophies. Red Head recognised the shape of his uncle but saw none of his features since he was coated from head to toe in red sand. They watched him disappear round the other bend at the far end of Ariel, leaning to the right with his pursuers at his shoulders.

The celebration was curbed by the arrival of the large pack of riders chasing Wheels and the bunch of leading riders. Blinding sand and noise confused and frightened the children. Seeing this monster with wheels that outnumbered the legs of a centipede fill Ariel's main road from one end to the next, raising more sand than the children thought covered the world, with a deafening tug and tear of tyre on sand, of chains through gears, over sprockets and brakes, made the children cling to adults.

Oblivious that it was in the middle of a race, the sandstorm took its time to pass Ariel. At last the sun brightened as if it had escaped through a hole in the wide net of red sand cast over it. Everyone ran into their houses and turned up their radios. Grandad assured them that the gap between the leaders and the pack giving chase was unbridge-able. He said Wheels was the best man with the best pair of legs and the most level head in that leading bunch and therefore, providing he kept his nerves under control, the race was his for the taking. Applause and cheers rang out.

Wheels had been picked up at 6 a.m. and driven in a jeep to the starting line by Raj's father, who was the only resident of Ariel with a motor vehicle. (The alternative would have been an even earlier start on the mule-drawn cart.) As soon as the last of the riders had passed, Bounce and Beanstalk had joined Raj's father for the drive to the finishing line to collect the champion. He was expected home around dusk. Granny had various pots bubbling on the wood stove, each emitting its own blend of spices and watering the children's mouths and driving them wild with distraction. The radio was so loud it could be heard anywhere in the house. The fast commentary said the foremost pack was due to meet the road builders soon, at which point the race was expected to pick up its pace, since the new road was smoother and faster than red sand.

Construction had come to a standstill a fortnight ago as the government negotiated more loans from the Interna-tional Monetary Fund and the World Bank. Newspapers and radios reported that work would not resume until after the election in another week's time. This left an itinerant community of workers and entertainers stranded around the silent machines and articulated trucks with nothing to do but gamble, drink and fight. A contingent of them had been summoned with promissory notes for their remunera-tion to clear the road under construction and facilitate the transition of the racing bikes from sand to bitumen. The disgruntled men had performed the chore haphazardly, pulling rakes half-heartedly over gravel, stamping on mounds that needed more determination if they were to be flattened at all, and decorating potholes with a few slaps and scrapes as if they were birthday cakes that had gone wrong and had to be rectified in a hurry.

Grandad was wrong about the gap between the leaders and the chasing pack. Rather than widening or even remaining the same, it narrowed. Since Ariel, the other men had settled behind Wheels, content for him to work at the front into a punishing head wind. He had decided not to go along with this and had slowed his pace to bring them up alongside him and to eat his sugar cake. By doing so he had unwittingly invited the chasing pack onto the shoulders of the leading group and now he was involved in a new battle to shake them off. The race approached the point where the road gang had put down their tools. Periodic attempts had been made to sprint away from the pack but the pack had simply clawed the leading riders back to it.

Once they hit the stretch of road under construction, the leading riders automatically slowed. They could feel the stones, mounds and dips in the road where potholes had been improperly filled. Smooth bitumen was only yards away but their bicycles slid from under them and the leaders crashed on top of each other. The pack bearing down on them tried to brake and steer round them but it had happened so fast they too collided and tumbled. Some riders ran off the road and into onlookers in an effort to avoid the pile-up. Others braked too hard, lost control and fell anyway, bringing down sections of the pack with them. A few men who would have come in last at the finish because they were trailing a couple of minutes behind the pack, braked in time and steered around the mangled bicycles, bruised riders and onlookers who had rushed to the aid of those who'd crashed. These few continued on to the capital as they marvelled at their good fortune.

'Harness the mule and cart.' Grandad put on his felt hat and Granny took off her apron. Footsy brought the mule and cart to them. They climbed aboard with Grandad holding the reins, which he slapped on the mule as he clicked his tongue. The children watched them until they disappeared at a trot. Footsy clanged about in the kitchen, stirring and tasting from the pots and inviting the children to sip from the steaming wooden spoon, but the aroma was gone from the house. Smoke, ash and sand seemed to permeate everything. Red Head tasted copper in his mouth so he sat in a corner, resting his head on his drawn-up legs, and rocked gently from side to side. Bash Man Goady asked him if he wanted to lie down. He declined with a shake of his head and a half-smile.

A traffic jam had formed behind the crash by vehicles following the race. Raj's father, Bounce and Beanstalk did not know what the hold-up was all about until word reached them that the race had been ruined by the new road. They left Raj's father in the jeep and ran the half-mile of vehicles stacked bumper to bumper. Horns blared and drivers shouted with their heads poked out of windows while they gesticulated with the passion of conductors without batons. They met a crowd. Beanstalk led the push through it. They found Wheels sitting on the roadside with his twisted bicycle next to him. He said he was fine though he was crying. He knew if he had had a second bicycle he could have completed the race. Some of the men who had crashed had abandoned their damaged bikes and mounted spare ones that were transported for them though most were too injured to continue or else they were in the same predicament as Wheels.

Beanstalk cleared a path for them back to the jeep. Wheels wanted to lie next to his bike in the back so Beanstalk and Bounce sat in the front with Raj's father, who drove and blinked rapidly to stem the flow of eye-water. Wheels lay on his back with his right forearm covering his face. They met Grandad and Granny. Both went to the jeep and hugged

Wheels and told him that when he passed in front of everyone as far as they were concerned he'd won. He was their champion.

When they got back to the house, the yard was full of people who clapped and cheered as Wheels climbed from the jeep. Everyone was careful to avoid the area around the guinep tree where Bubble Back and Double Back slept ignorant of the crowd. Wheels thanked his neighbours and began to limp to the house but was swept off his feet and onto the shoulders of a few men nearby and borne right up to the veranda, where they deposited him as delicately as a flower. Wings was propped against the porch, each letter of its hand-painted name trailed in clearly discernible flames despite a preponderance of scratches and sand. Grandad thanked the crowd and beckoned his family inside. Then the yard emptied, leaving the mule standing harnessed to the cart, shifting its weight from leg to leg and gazing at the field where it was usually let loose to graze.

Singh v. Singh 2

'EASY. EASY. EASY,' crackled his supporters on the transistor radio as Singh gave his post-mortem on the precise nature of the knot he'd tied his latest opponent in, more as a guide for his assistants at ringside to undo, going by his slow articulation, than as a boast. Bounce sat in his customary pose, his back straight, his eyes trained on a spot two feet in front of him. He swayed as Grandad massaged his neck and shoulders.

'I am not an Indian wrestler. I am a wrestler from India.'

The government had accorded the lowest possible priority to Singh's visit, not even bothering to throw the mandatory reception for an entertainer of his stature. Their excuse that they were too busy electioneering concluded, 'He should not inform us when he is coming, we should instruct him when it suits us for him to visit.' The opposition leader who met a bewildered Singh at the airport by sheer coincidence had rearranged his schedule to free some of his men and vehicles for Singh's transportation to a hotel and had sponsored a welcoming reception, hastily organised, by begging local grocery stores and restaurants loyal to his party to pledge the food and drink. These shopkeepers could hardly afford to give but they were too much in love with *their* President to refuse his requests. The impromptu reception turned the opposition leader into 'the great facilitator' in the eyes of small business and earned each sponsor free tickets to Singh's matches.

With each bout Singh's support swelled as his opponents'

fans defected. Once Singh became national news, the government offered him 'irresistible terms' for his support and he accepted. Now he was their election campaign. Though no speeches were made by government ministers, every wrestling match was an election rally as Singh's adversaries became aligned with the opposition who could do nothing but look and curse Singh duplicity, and worry about the efficacy of their own campaign without Singh on their side. Trucks working days supplying the road gang were chartered into Singh supporter carriers at night. At first one truck, named in big letters along the sides 'No Time to Lose', was sufficient to ferry Singh, his manager, trainer, publicist, dresser, barber and three seconds who doubled as bodyguards, along with their equipment of buckets, sponges, grease, talcum powder, towels, a handful of women admirers and various floor-length satin capes with high collars in the glorious colours of the rainbow. He entered the arena with one draped over his shoulders. His seconds would prise the ropes apart with their hands and feet to enable him to walk into the ring. The cape was then ceremoniously swung over his head moments before the starting bell for the contest. Other personal effects, such as a variety of aftershaves, gumshields, placards reading, 'Easy', 'Pushover', 'No Sweat' and 'Joke' that were held up by his assistants to prompt the crowd's chant, balm that gave his hair the sheen of a mirror held to the sun and kept it plastered to his skull regardless of how many cartwheels he did around his opponent, a hundred yards of waxed bootlace to replace the ones that snapped in his ten pairs of calf-length boots, a manicure set for his nails, handlebar moustache and wide sideburns that almost met the corners of his mouth, a black dye to suppress the speckle of grey hairs in both, and a medicine chest full of Andrew's Liver Salts and laxatives disguised as chocolate bars were closely guarded by his attendants against saboteurs. One had injected strychnine into a laxative bar which was eaten by a new girlfriend taken on board Singh's tour who had mistaken it for dark chocolate, no longer available because of a government ban on luxury imports intended to promote the inferior local brands. She had died within twenty-nine minutes of her feast, luckily before the laxative took effect.

The news of an opponent whose ancestry included not only African and Indian blood but Portuguese, too, over-joyed him. Just before the Ariel bout his convoy of trucks had reached ten. Their names were drawn from every conceivable source: Fireball 500, She's Gone Again, Easy Rider, Bluebird, Hummingbird, Thunderbird, Doubletake, Roadrunner and Lightning.

'You are next, he won't need all those trucks. Just one to transport the aspirin for that big headache you're going to give to him,' Grandad asserted, after the news that featured Singh and nothing else. Everyone applauded the announce-ment of Bounce's name on the radio and masked their fear for him as the praise heaped on Singh and his unbeaten run transformed him into a ten-foot giant with hands that could bend men and iron bars and plait them like dough.

Ariel saw one of its rare generators when a truck called Second to None arrived with the dismantled wrestling ring. Beanstalk was hired along with some other local men to help set up the generator, ring and floodlights. When the govern-ment engineer said he would have to determine the centre of the field where Ariel's film shows took place, Beanstalk pointed it out to him to save time. The man ignored Beanstalk and proceeded to mount an instrument on a tripod. He made a neat drawing of the field, took measurements from three different points in it, did numerous calculations and one hour later ended up where Beanstalk had indicated.

A crowd of onlookers watched as the men cleared the ground and sank four posts into it. Four taller posts with lights and wires dangling from them were erected behind the first four. The ring's foundation was comprised of a wooden platform raised about three feet off the ground. A foam mat was unrolled onto the wood floor, stretched, nailed and taped in place. A canvas sheet, similarly stretched and secured, covered the foam. Three ropes about a foot apart were then strung between the four posts. The engineer threw his weight against the ropes to test their security. They yielded like elastic and he seemed about to fall out of the ring but then they appeared to soak up his propelled body and contract and toss him to the canvas. He signalled all was as it should be by thrusting his right hand into the air with his index finger and thumb formed into an O and the other three fingers spread out. Four soldiers took up positions around the ring to prevent people from even touching it. The generator was tested and the lights popped on and off. Ariel had its first, brief experience of electricity, not counting the projector that showed it films. Another soldier stationed himself next to the generator. An assistant to the engineer paid everyone. Those who had arrived that morning climbed into Second to None and left for the capital, except for five unsmiling soldiers in dark glasses, with berets pulled low over their eyes against the afternoon sun. Beanstalk took one last look at the ring and at the position of the lights before he left for home with his wages jingling in his pocket.

Grandad, Wheels and Bounce met Beanstalk at the front gate. Anyone who did not belong to the family was asked to leave the property. Strategy, Grandad said and they understood instantly. Raj and Sten waved goodbye and left with Raj's father and two other men from the rum shop, one of whom had just finished shaving Bounce's head. Using the stick of sage he'd broken off to chew on his walk home, Beanstalk drew a life-sized model of the ring and the position of the lights in the red sand. Grandad placed a chair in a corner of the square and got Bounce to walk from the chair to the centre of the makeshift ring in a set number of steps with his eyes closed. He next made Bounce practise this short walk from each of the corners. Then he stood Beanstalk, believed to be Singh's height, in the middle and asked Bounce to approach from a corner as before. Bounce closed his eyes and stepped forward. He stopped a foot from his brother, who towered fourteen inches above him. He opened his eyes and his gaze locked with Beanstalk's. Beanstalk turned his head as if from a piercing light, rocked back on his heels and fell to the ground. Bounce helped him to his feet and they hugged. Grandad shushed all the cries of amazement from the rest of the family and ordered everyone into the house to sleep for the remainder of the afternoon. The entire ground floor was vacated for Bounce and his brothers and Grandad.

The children lying on the floor above could hear whispering. They recognised Grandad's voice but failed to identify exactly which of the others belonged to whom. Red Head located the spot on the floor where Grandad sounded. Bash Man Goady marked the other two voices with rolled-up sheets. The three points they'd mapped formed a proper triangle. One voice was missing. They worked out it was located in the middle of the triangle and that Bounce occupied it. When the whispers subsided they found themselves listening to each other's even breathing or else the empty stillness of the afternoon and they dozed.

A spy, foolish and therefore brave enough to look in on that ground floor, would see the old man in the hammock, made from ripped-out flour sacks and called Yellow Submarine, with his hat on his face; Beanstalk on his back on a straw mat with his arms folded behind his head; Wheels lying on his side, the healing left side uppermost; and Bounce seated in a half-lotus, hands resting on his knees, straight-backed, eyes shut and immovable. The square drawn in the sand would escape the spy's notice or be dismissed as the remnants of a children's game. He would have nothing to report, but, like all spies who resent going back empty-handed, he might embellish the scene. The young man with the big head would be credited with a neck as large as a man's thigh and with shoulders comparable to a bull's front haunches, necessary if that head and neck were to remain vertical. If these distinguishing features were the identifying marks of a good wrestler, then he'd be a serious challenger, but to this spy they'd be deemed as the malformations there to compensate for the most outstanding of them all: a really big head. From the evidence before his eyes the spy would be led to one conclusion: the challenge is a joke.

'Joke. Joke. Joke,' chanted the crowd of government supporters. The field was full. Those nearest to the ring were bathed in a pool of white light swimming with confused insects. They outnumbered Ariel citizens loyal to Bounce by ten to one.

Raj and his father with his extended family stood beside Sten and her parents and five sisters. Red Head and his brother joined them with all the children and aunts and uncles from the house. Only Granny had stayed at home to prepare what she called a victory dinner. Grandad positioned himself in front of Bounce, who sat on the edge of a stool in the corner of the ring. He held his son's head in his hands and spoke to him. His face was thrust so close to Bounce's that their noses almost touched and it blotted the crowd from Bounce's sight. Bounce breathed heavily and fast like he did as a child when about to cry. 'Stop breathing in your neck, son. Take air to the pit of your stomach, then fill up to your collarbone.' Bounce blinked and his breathing slowed. 'Don't let him grab you and lift you off the ground. Wait for him to move before you strike, no matter how long he takes, wait.'

Beanstalk and Wheels acted as seconds. They stood

outside the ropes, close to their bent father and seated brother, facing the crowd and glaring at anyone who tried to get near Bounce to insult him to his face. If someone who was unfamiliar to them shouted encouragement, they nodded in appreciation. Otherwise they surveyed the crowd, whose chants were guided by placards held up by an assistant of Singh's.

Singh was nowhere to be seen. A doctor and referee consulted in a corner and glanced at their watches: three minutes to eight. 'Pushover' was written on the placard held up in the light. Those able to read shouted 'Pushover' and the crowd took up the chant. 'Pushover. Pushover. Pushover.'

Red Head jumped to his feet, cupped his hand to his mouth and shouted at his relatives, 'Bounce, Bounce,' and clapped three times in rapid succession. Footsy was about to grab him and sit him on the grass next to her when he stepped out of her reach and again shouted 'Bounce' twice and clapped three times. Bash Man Goady, Raj, Sten and the other children took up the calling and clapping. The adults fell in with them. Grandad gave them the thumbs-up. This had the effect of quietening the majority of the crowd, who had chanted without opposition until now. They recovered when a few of them substituted Singh for Bounce and copied the exact sequence of calls and claps initiated by Red Head.

The referee looked at his watch about the same time as Grandad and everyone else who had one to read. Eight o'clock. According to the rules Singh had three minutes to materialise or forfeit the match. Singh never appeared before the last seconds of the time limit were on the lips of the crowd.

Grandad straightened and touched Bounce's arms. Bounce sprang to his feet. His brothers pulled the stool from the ring. 'Close your eyes.'

Bounce obeyed. He heard his name fade and a countdown

from ten begin. It was like day from the light that shone behind his clamped lids. Cheers rose from the dark edges of the crowd and grew louder as Singh danced his way to the ring and dodged the many hands held out to touch him. At five seconds his assistants had trapped the lowest rope of the ring under their feet. At four they had raised the upper two above their heads. At three the tall, strapping figure of Singh glistened at ringside. At two, he hopped the three feet up to the opening made for him. At one, he ducked into the ring, swung his cape above his head, then threw it at an assistant and shuffled his feet on the canvas. The crowd stamped on the grass, screamed, shouted, clapped and whistled. The referee flicked his watch back into his fob pocket with palpable relief, not wanting to be the one who would have had to enforce the rules and inform the crowd that Singh had been disqualified, had he been late by another second.

The doctor and referee looked at Singh's nails and envied them their manicure. They glanced at the bottom of his red leather boots. The long black laces and tassels were sprayed with glitter. Singh removed a world-championship belt from his waist and pulled up his shorts. When they came over to Bounce and saw his bare feet, both got to their hands and knees to examine each toenail individually. Parts of the crowd went quiet because they thought the two were paying homage to Bounce. They asked Grandad if Bounce was asleep or drugged or in a trance. Grandad said closing his eyes kept his son's concentration from wavering. They called Bounce's name as a test and he answered with a growl that caused them to raise their eyebrows.

The referee ordered everyone who should not be there to leave the ring right away. Grandad told Bounce to make him even prouder than he'd already made him, then he ducked through the ropes and stood beside his two other sons. Both the doctor and Singh's assistants copied Grandad but went to the opposite corner at ringside. The referee signalled the two combatants to approach him. Sweat covered Bounce. Singh looked at his opponent for the first time. Singh, whose eyes never lied to him, eyes that immobilised guard dogs by glaring at them or silenced crying children with a glance, saw a head that resembled a battering ram and a body that was a smaller, younger version of himself. His smile dissolved. When his gaze travelled along the mallet-shaped head and met the eyes anchored in it, he jumped into a defensive stance. The crowd hushed. Singh's assistants leaned on the ropes to see what had spooked the conqueror, the pacifier, the undefeated, the magnificent. They saw two red sources of light which shone with menace.

The radio commentator said Singh faced his young self, a case of Singh versus Singh. As the referee explained the need for a clean fight to Singh and Bounce, the two stared each other in the eyes without blinking. Singh had his right foot about six inches in front of his left. His knees were bent. Both arms were raised to chest level and his fingers were spread and curled a little. He gritted his teeth, though from a distance it looked like a smile. If he straightened his arms he would touch his opponent. Bounce had his left hand at chest level and his right hand waist-high. His fingers were spread out and straight, making his hands look much bigger than their actual size. His lips were sealed and whitened from the pressure applied to them.

The referee's shout of 'Wrestle' combined with the bell was loud and clear, revivifying the audience's cheers and shouts. Both men remained glued to the spot, eyes locked. Red Head looked at Grandad, who was watching his son and nodding in approval. Neither man lunged for the other nor even moved to another part of the ring; in fact, neither man twitched or blinked. After urging Singh to convert Bounce into all manner of knots, shapes and angles, the audience went quiet. Some jeered and booed, others laughed. Still the two athletes faced each other, statuesque in their stillness.

When the bell sounded for the end of the first round and both men maintained their stance, it suddenly dawned on the audience that a monumental battle of wills was under way. The referee knew the rules had been flouted but he retreated shivering. He was the closest soul to those two pairs of eyes and their combined power had drained the energy from him. People pressed closer to the ropes to get a better view after the word 'eyes' uttered by one group of mouths had passed to another group and in its repetition by so many took on the quality of a mantra.

The bell for round two to begin sounded superfluous. Both men were drenched in sweat. It dropped off their chins and elbows, cascaded down their naked torsos and soaked their shorts, and ran into pristine boots and between bare toes. The radio commentator asked his listeners to note that something of historical importance was transpiring right there in the Cooperative Republic village number —— of Ariel and he would summon everything to convey it to them, but they should note that it came from him first.

Round three. 'Singh, Singh,' followed by three claps, began with a difference. It was directed at both men. Mesmerised by the quality of Singh's opposition the crowd loyal to Singh and the government completely forgot its function as rabble-rousers and actually expressed a desire for the best man to win. Grandad noticed Singh's eyelid on his left eye drop a fraction. It had been weakened years ago when an unexpected blow from the handbag of an enraged mother of a defeated opponent in a London bout had completely detached the retina, necessitating an operation. He saluted the air, turned to his two sons and whispered that they should prepare to leave in a hurry. The eyelid fell another fraction and obscured a slice of the iris. A slight tremor was discernible in Singh's hands because they were two feet from a pair of hands that were composed. At the bell for the end of round three, a quarter of the iris was covered and everyone at ringside saw and began to whisper to those further back. By round four, three quarters of the eye was covered. All that was visible was a slice of white in the lower part of the eye. Then the eyelid flickered and clamped shut. Singh's hands twitched and Bounce took this as his signal to strike.

Not a soul in that field was able to follow with the naked eye the forward trajectory of Bounce's head. They heard the crack of a whip or that of an axe splitting dry wood. They saw Singh fly backwards with only his heels in contact with the canvas as if a lasso had been flung around his waist and an invisible horseman riding upside down along the ceiling of the sky was dragging him. Singh toppled over the top of the ropes and crashed to the ground. The crowd gasped. The air in the field contracted and burned the lungs and constricted the hearts of all those who sucked on it.

Singh's assistants leapt to him and lifted him under the bottom rope and rolled the sack of flesh and bones into the ring. The referee began his count, slower than any clock as though he did not recognise the numbers in his head but said them anyway. Bounce did not move, not even his eyes. At the count of ten, the bell rang and the referee waved both arms as if flagging down a speeding motorist at the scene of an accident. Singh's men ran to his side to rescue him from the land of the fairies. They called Singh, Singh, Singh, but, instead of clapping, slapped his face. Nothing. Smelling salts were held under his nose by the doctor. Still nothing. His ears were pinched, then bitten. Not a flutter. The doctor listened to Singh's chest, then held Singh's wrist with three middle fingers and studied the second hand of his watch. He shrugged. He ordered the men to remove the boot from Singh's right foot. They used a knife to cut through the lace and yanked the boot off. The doctor ran the top of a pen from Singh's big toe to his heel. Singh's toes curled. This pleased the doctor. 'He's alive but he's in a coma.' Transistors hummed and crackled up and down the land as the commentator stared voiceless from Bounce to the supine Singh, then back at Bounce.

Grandad said, 'Everyone home fast.' He grabbed Bounce by his arm. Bounce shook him off and went to the sleeping wrestler. Singh's attendants and the doctor recoiled from Singh and opened a gap for the massive head's approach. Bounce knelt, leaned close to the legendary ear and whispered. Singh stirred. Bounce retreated to his father and winked at his brothers who flanked him. They began to force a path through the crowd with the children and aunts close behind. Sten and Raj's parents retreated to their houses too.

Singh clawed his head and screamed, suddenly conscious of a helmet that gradually tightened. His men tried to hold his arms to stop him removing further handfuls of hair. Singh threw them out of the ring or tied them in a knot that left them in a ball on the canvas. More men poured in, begging Singh to stop before he was completely bald. He paused either to eject them over the ropes or to fashion them into boneless-looking shapes. At last the doctor plunged a needle into Singh's leg and the giant became slower and slower until he toppled under the weight of ten men and cried himself into a drugged sleep.

The House on Red Sand

'COUNT THE CHILDREN. Lock the doors and bolt the windows.' Grandad fired instructions at everyone in sight.

Granny led Bounce to a chair. He sat in a stupor and tugged his earlobes and his lips, pinched his nose and plucked his eyebrows and head to verify that all were in fact on his shoulders. For the first time in his life the weight of his world of migraines had been lifted off his back, creating the illusion that his neck no longer supported anything. He could do nothing but sit and wonder at his new condition. His brothers and sisters dashed around him as they fortified the house. They stacked heavy furniture against the windows and doors, leaving one side window and one door free as possible escape routes. Cutlasses and long sticks were handed to all the adults. Bounce gave the club laid next to him to Bash Man Goady. 'I won't need that,' he said, pointing to his skull, 'I have one of my own.'

Bash Man Goady lifted it with both hands.

'Anyone come near you and your brother, lick them with it.'

Bash Man Goady nodded and positioned himself in front of Red Head. He held the club as if he were standing at a cricket crease about to hit the ball to the boundary.

Red Head whispered at him, 'You can relax till they reach here.'

Bash Man Goady retorted, 'Shut up and stay behind me or I'll use it on you.'

Singh was carried by six men to No Time to Lose and laid in the trailer among all his accoutrements. His assistants were crying and asking everyone near them how this terrible thing could happen to their great Singh. Singh was destined to win. The government supporters were supposed to throw an all-night party afterwards. They had arrived as the inevitable victors and no amount of assuagement could make palatable their new role as the vanquished. Others revived and released the twenty or so men Singh had tied into a variety of postures. Someone shouted, 'They work obeah on Singh.' More information about Bounce and his family was volunteered from all quarters of the crowd, now beginning to recover from the lightning blow that had stunned it too. 'The tallest one can fly backwards over a six-foot fence.' 'Another one can ride round a track so fast he give bird eye turn.' 'One of them come from the Amerindian tribe that eat people and make flutes with their bones.' 'The opposition own that Bounce.'

They began to tear the ring down, helped by the soldiers. A few of Ariel's residents who had not managed to make themselves scarce were beaten unconscious. The platform was broken into pieces and the ropes around the ring cut to shreds. The four posts with lights were pulled down and the generator spluttered and died. In the darkness lit by a few lanterns and the headlights of trucks parked on the road, foam and canvas were torn and attached to sticks which were doused with petrol from the trucks and the torches distributed among them. The crowd marched towards Bounce's house, arming themselves with posts and staves ripped from the fences of houses they passed along the way.

They paused at Sabbatic's house to confirm that the mockery of singing sailing out of its many apertures was indeed that of a pathetic drunk and not taunts from a sympathiser of Bounce. A man at the front of the crowd threw his kerosene lamp into the windowless house anyway.

The glass shade crashed like cymbals but the lamp did not spill its contents. A tall, thin figure appeared at one of the openings that birds flew through on their way to somewhere. He held the lit lamp aloft, minus its shade. The crowd braced themselves, thinking he might throw the lamp back at them. But Sabbatic drained the kerosene into his mouth, appeared to eat the lit wick, then spat a fifteen-foot flame into the night air, illuminating a sea of startled faces, the rickety house and his bony features in as little time as a struck match takes to flare. The crowd shrank from the house. The man who threw the lamp waved his fist and shouted at Sabbatic that he'd be back for it in the morning. Sabbatic pelted the lamp at the man and told him not to bring it half-empty but filled with kerosene next time. One of the soldiers aimed and fired twice at Sabbatic before the others grabbed his gun and told him to save his bullets for the real troublemakers. The window where Sabbatic had stood and vilified the crowd framed an empty square that leaked darkness and silence.

At the sound of gunshots Bounce shook off his reverie and got into a circle with his two brothers and Granny and Grandad. He was explaining something they wouldn't agree to when the noise of the approaching crowd interrupted. As the aunts hurried the children to the back of the house, Red Head called out, 'Bounce can save us.' The circle opened and faced Red Head. Granny asked him what he meant. He said he had a dream. There was red and then there was black. Only Bounce could guide them through the red. Red for blood and black for bodies. Red flowed from the black. 'Only Bounce can save us.' Footsy guided him to the back of the house, closing every door behind them.

The log bridge thundered. This was not the noise of a donkey and loaded cart crossing the logs laid loosely side by side from the road over the trench and into the front yard, but a stampede. Palings next to the gate were uprooted and the gate demolished with axes and kicks and tugs. Red Head ran to see out of the side window designated as an emergency escape route but Footsy caught him by his waist. He protested that Sten, her sisters and parents were coming. Grandad opened it just a crack and by the way he leaned his forehead against it everyone knew it was true. Lamps flickered about halfway between the two houses. An end portion of the crowd noticed the lights too and detached itself from the main body with the specific intention of extinguishing those lights and the souls bearing them.

'Is me you want.'

The men in the yard halted.

'Not my family or anybody else.'

They raised their torches to see who was shouting at them.

Bounce opened the front door. 'I coming.' He stood at the door in the shadowy, dancing light of the fires. Beanstalk and Wheels slipped out the back and into the consuming darkness. Red Head felt water sting his eyes for Sten and her sisters and parents and uncles. The small section of the crowd heading for the field broke into a run, shouting and whistling. Granny stood by the window with her back to it to prevent the children from witnessing what she found unthinkable. Red Head lay on the floor and peered through one of the holes made by the bullets from the previous attack. His cyclops view captured the unmoving lamps from Sten's family in its right corner, while in its left a group of naked flames charged and reduced the darkness separating the two sets of lights. Red Head was about to close his eye as the edges of the different lights mingled when a lamp flickered to life in that dully lit gap. The charging group of flames halted. He worked out from the height of the lamp that Beanstalk carried it. There was no movement for the longest while. The fires seemed to be considering their different existences – one open to the air, big and wild, the other shaded, small and controlled. Then the lamps of Sten's family began to advance again, guided by Beanstalk's single lamp and tracked by the flames of the crowd.

Bounce stepped onto the porch and into the yard. The men at the front of the crowd raised their sticks and torches. Others were trying to push their way from the main road to see why their progress to the house had stopped. Bounce focused on a point about three feet ahead. He asked the soldiers not to shoot, he couldn't fight bullets. 'I trained in the ricefield to fight men.'

His shaven head in the poor light of their torches confounded their attempts to identify him. They saw the offending head but not the boyish features decorating it. He had to be eradicated along with the offence, not simply against Singh and their government, but against all their expectations and frustrations. Bounce may have sensed that very thing when he declared his intent to fight instead of any show of bargaining or begging for their mercy. They waited for something to be said by him or anyone else that might alleviate the tension of knowing what had to be done next and not wanting to begin an act of such finality. Bounce had offered himself to them by his emergence from the house, yet from their hesitancy it seemed as if they were the ones up for sacrifice.

One man spat at Bounce. Others began to spit too. Bounce did nothing to evade them. The men further back elbowed their way forwards so that they could spit as well. Saliva ran off Bounce's face and body. Those who were hemmed in too far back to advance, craned their necks and spat into the air, hoping it would travel the few rows over their friends and somehow reach Bounce. Those at the front started to get drenched from behind. A few looked back and saliva caught them square in the face. Hands raised to call a cessation to the spitting just drew more fire and became so covered they were retracted. Bounce smiled. They charged. Bounce struck, not once or twice but several times in succession. Each blow from his head sounded with such rapidity only a drum roll could have matched it. He took small steps back. Bodies crumpled at his feet. He ignored the lashes from sticks and the stones pelted at him. When a flung torch connected, he wiped the sediment of oil and fire from him and tore off his clothes. His head maintained its drum roll and he his gradual retreat.

Sten's father raised his cutlass for Wheels and Beanstalk to see. More than thirty men faced them. They were poised about fifty yards from the house. Granny opened the back door and called to them. The girls and their mother began to run. The men swung their staves and cutlasses at Wheels, Beanstalk and Sten's father. Bones cracked and broke. Wood lashed against flesh. Teeth flew. Blood flowed. The razor grass began to burn with abandoned torches. A few of the men got past Sten's father, Wheels and Beanstalk and closed on the girls and their mother. Sten's mother glanced over her shoulder and stopped and shouted at the girls to keep running. She turned and faced the men with her two fists raised like a boxer. Grandad ran past the girls with Footsy and another of his daughters, all carrying cutlasses. Granny slammed the door behind the girls, who fell to the floor screaming and leaned on it. She shouted at them and they clamped their mouths shut and whimpered. Red Head and Bash Man Goady led them to the back room where all the children were gathered.

Flames from the field lit the house. Smoke crept under the door of the veranda. Shots were heard at the front of the house. A loud cry rose from the men. The front door was rammed again and again. Two aunts and Granny picked up the kitchen knives and rolling pins and the smooth wooden pestle used to pound yam in a mortar. They told the children to open the back door if they recognised the voice, otherwise they were not to move, then they rushed to the front door.

By crawling around the room on their bellies the children were able to collect used matches and splinters of wood. They dressed half of the used matches with discarded pink chewing gum and called them the heads and stood the matches on their opposite ends. A matchbox or bottletop was designated a car. The girls controlled the pink-haired matches, the boys the matches with cropped black hair and the cars. Red Head was lucky to find a match that had not been used. He called the round sulphur end an afro. The boys crawled around the room pushing their matchboxes and bottletops with their matchsticks in them and hummed engine sounds. They met their pink-haired girlfriends who had a tendency to stick to them or their cars. Kissing proved especially difficult. If the lovers came apart suddenly because some of the children jumped at a scream that was near or a scream they recognised, then the black-haired match would be covered in pink chewing gum and the girl would be left embarrassingly hairless. Smoke drifted under the door. Some of the children coughed. Sten's pink-haired woman stormed off from Red Head's man with the afro. She pecked the floor rapidly with the matchstick, creating the effect of six-inch heels. Red Head drove his bottletop and implored her to climb aboard. She stood still, considered it for a moment, and clambered in. They drove the bottletop together, parked and forced their lovers into such a long embrace, it would require some ingenuity to separate them without the lady losing her hair.

II

Nightmares from

the Republic of Dreams

The Pages of the Sea

Brukup arrived at the capital's sea wall on his fixed-wheel bicycle. His shrivelled legs pedalled along the jetty. He reached his usual point of departure from land at 6 p.m. on the dot and flopped into the sea for his daily swim. His regular audience, with one or two new onlookers, shook their heads at the spectacle. An inclination to prop the bike upright on its stand was quashed by a host of dissenting voices. Touch 'the thing', as the bike was called, interrupt that spinning back wheel and the tick of that well-greased sprocket, and Brukup will be back to contend with you. It had happened before and it would happen again. Just leave 'the thing' alone and enjoy the spectacle.

There was Brukup in his half-frail form braving the undertow of the evening tide when most strapping young men admitted they were afraid. They preferred to court girls on the solid side of the concrete and marvel at Brukup.

'The man jump in the sea with he briefcase.'

'As if it not hard enough to swim without legs.'

'Brukup working overtime while he swimming.' Their curiosity degenerated into ribaldry.

'Is not a briefcase, is a life jacket in disguise.'

'No, the thing have a engine to help him swim.'

Once Brukup was sure he was too far out to be seen, he stopped his propeller arms. One arm treaded water oddly like a synchronised swimmer practising without a partner. Now he appeared to be gutting a fish as his other arm unzipped the briefcase while he gripped the handle between his teeth and he pulled and spilled white papers from its black leather and tossed them like discarded entrails on the tide. Before speeding towards the lights that beckoned him with their winking to return to the shore, Brukup lay on his back and stared in concentration or meditation at the sky, blackened by star-obscuring cloud. Had his incompetent colleague Gamediser been delegated the same responsibility, Brukup was convinced that Gamediser, short of eating the papers, would almost certainly have complicated the task of disposing of them, with another of his famous errors as well as with twice the fuss. He couldn't fathom why the President tolerated Gamediser's perspiring bulk around him. Brukup pictured Gamediser and refashioned his rival's prodigious, land-locked mass into a seafaring tanker, one of those quarter-mile-long oil carriers which take several miles to alter course by a fraction. Brukup was Neptune. He reared from the water waist-high, grabbed the tanker that was a mere toy to him and snapped it in two. He sank back to his head above the sea and watched the broken tanker emit a million bubbles as it disappeared into the murky deep of his subconsciousness.

From floating on his back like a plank adrift, Brukup changed his position to upright. Were his head fluorescent, bobbing as it was, it would have made a perfect buoy. He eased his shorts down and performed his customary bowel movement. It was good. Bowel contents chased briefcase contents to the sea bed. Then he pointed himself towards the jetty. The action seemed to pull a cord on an outboard motor. His mighty arms propelled him towards the beckoning lights of the shore.

At the jetty, Brukup heaved his torso out of the sea and felt instant displeasure, as he always did, at the way it readily took on the burden of gravity. He pulled and pushed against gravity all day except for the brief respite of his nightly swim, when it eased and he felt the equal of any man. He answered the questioning faces as he peeled off his wet vest and shorts, and, still in a sitting position, climbed into dry trousers and a shirt that were in his saddle bag. 'All you think I stupid because I look stupid, like I ain't got no topside or something and would leave my valuables.'

His muscle-bound arms and shoulders snatched the bike upright as if he'd bent down for a twig. Rotating his hips, he picked up his leg and threw it over the cross-bar. His red tail-light glowed as he pedalled and the dynamo whined against the tyre. The couples strolled on and the few people who idled on the jetty, just to see Brukup, talked some more about Brukup before they dispersed. One of them asked, 'What can he do for the government that I can't do?'

Heavy traffic passed Brukup on the new road. Those who wanted to feel what it was like to be driven on new bitumen were ferried by taxis the few miles out of the capital to within sight of the work gang and its burgeoning city, and back again. Trucks raced to and from the creeping construction site with their commissioned supplies. Donkey-drawn carts with lanterns hanging from them brought whatever the local village had to sell to the work gang, fresh fruit for the most part or the speciality of the village, which was anything from dhal puree to black pudding, pepperpot or teenage prostitutes. Motorcycles visited the road gang with sweethearts brought by their protective brothers to see fiancés who were contracted to it, and with friends who came to see those who'd succeeded in getting the coveted job of making the country's arterial road navigable without breaking an axle or getting marooned in sand when it rained.

The capital's best-known polio victim cursed when the bitumen road ran out and he hit the potholed red sand he couldn't wait to see disappear. Two huge sores on his rump ruptured. Usually, pain from them aggravated him throughout the day. He had to carry a special cushion seat wherever he went. His bicycle saddle was customised with insulation to minimise the pressure on the lesions. The pain that had been banished temporarily as a result of his soak in tidal salt water stormed through him when he hit those potholes and vandalised beyond recognition the pleasant thoughts he was entertaining. These thoughts were in part to blame for his carelessness. He was so engrossed in them he had failed to register in his mind the evidence of his eyes, namely that the new road was about to end. Had he clocked that fact he would have used his enormous arms to pull his bottom off the saddle so that when he hit the red sand those powerful shock absorbers gripping the handle-bar would mean he would not have felt the biggest bump or deepest rut.

But no, he was thinking about victories, congratulating himself on how easy it had been to destroy those vital papers so many very powerful people had urged him to lose permanently. He'd veered from his usual policy of 'what you don't know can't hurt you' by sneaking a look at the papers. What he had seen had made him shove them back in his briefcase and take them to the jetty pronto. So quick, in fact, he had to take a detour which added another quarter of a mile to his journey, in order not to arrive early for his swim and perhaps arouse the suspicion of the regular bystanders.

He'd read the shortened minutes of meetings between the President and a clutch of cabinet ministers and a number of memos they'd exchanged. He was about to read the budgets for the venture and the names of those agents, as they were called, who were directly involved, when he decided he'd seen enough. All were concerned with the overseas vote and how these could be procured. Not in the usual electioneering sense of won or secured, but 'invented'. That was the word which had caused the minutes and memos to be inadmissible, according to the reasoning of the government, to the archives. It was Brukup's task as a courier of these important papers to ensure that they never got into the hands of the archivist. He had executed these instructions to the letter: all the papers about the overseas-votes initiative were indeed now undersea. The seabed would be their archive.

A rare smile had begun to play on his lips. Completely forgetting to brace himself for the transition from runway-smooth bitumen to wheel-buckling sand, he took the full impact of the first pothole on his two incurable sores. When he gathered himself off the saddle with a powerful heave on the handlebar, in his panic he must have tugged too hard. The front wheel rocketed out of the pothole (helped by the rim of the hole, which had an effect much like the upward curve of the end of a ramp) and should have been sucked back down to terra firma by the pull of gravity almost immediately, had it not been for Brukup's arms that were holding it up. Instead, the wheel kept rising. Brukup fought to keep his balance by doing two things: first, he pedalled as hard as he could with his flimsy legs; second, he pushed down on the handlebar. This kept him from falling but he travelled for several yards with the front wheel high off the ground. The men in the work gang dropped their hammers and shovels, pickaxes and hoes, and applauded, whistled, guffawed, punched the air and slapped their thighs. Brukup transferred all his will to his arms and pressed on the handlebars. The front wheel hit the sand with such force that the tyre exploded. Several spokes on the wheel pinged like guitar strings and the wheel buckled. Brukup tightened the vice of his hands on the handlebars and pedalled, determined to escape the jeering work gang. But the power of his arms had remoulded the front wheel into a rough sphere which wobbled, rose and fell, as he rode. Laughter from the workmen reached a new pitch. Brukup pedalled beyond the glare of the floodlights. He felt like a circus clown who'd just left the ring on his joke bike. Back in the dark he cursed aloud to drown out the laughter behind him. 'Nothing can ruin tonight,' he told the thickening dark. The various generators at the roadworks, the engines, the raucous laughter, all subsided and were succeeded by a different orchestra: the twang of broken spokes tangled between the wheel, frog croaks, cricket chirps, the occasional volley from a guard or stray dog, and the braying of a donkey. Brukup's legs burned for some respite from the gruelling ride, but he knew if he stopped it would be impossible to push the bicycle with its spherical front wheel and mangled tyre and walk on his spindle legs.

Brukup turned into the yard of Belinda's. He decided that he needed to be consoled after his recent humiliation. He threw down the bike and sneered at it. His sneer deepened when he transferred his gaze from the bike to his wobbly legs. His knees stopped knocking, called to attention by the reproachful look of a frightful drill sergeant. At the door were a dozen or so children waiting for their mothers who were working inside; he asked one of them if Belinda was around. A little girl with knotted blond hair, in a faded cotton dress whose hem she obviously chewed when upset or tired, said Belinda was away on business. The child seemed agitated, shifting her weight from one foot to the other. Her bare feet were stockinged in red sand. Brukup estimated her age at six or seven. His stern glance made the child start to chew on the hem of her dress. Brukup wished she would twist a little more of the cotton print around her thumb, for that would lift it the extra couple of inches he needed to confirm whether she had panties on or not. Fifty to one against, he speculated. He made his expression a bit more severe, nearer to a scowl. The girl stepped back from him and water sprang to her eyes. Brukup quickly dug into his pocket and dropped three coins into her hands which she cupped, still clutching her dress, and raised towards him. Her face blossomed with this smile that was so broad and bright it caused Brukup's own face, involuntarily, to follow suit. Other children ran forward, some to see how much their friend had made, some with doleful looks on their faces hoping to inspire more charity in the crooked-looking man. After he'd turned from her with his practised smile fading, Brukup realised he'd forgotten his small wager. The remains of the smile crumbled and his sneer re-attached itself to his face.

A waitress approached Brukup as he walked in his fashion towards the bar. Before she could ask for his order, 'his delight' was how Belinda had trained them to put it, Brukup made it clear without looking at her that he wanted Tracy, nobody else, just Tracy. The waitress told him Tracy was busy for a while and asked whether he'd like a drink in the meantime. 'No, but you have one, here.' He flicked ten dollars on her tray. She beamed at him and shouted over the talk and laughter in the room to the barman to find a low stool for the kind gentleman. Brukup jerked his right shoulder towards his ear, which lifted, and swung his hips forwards, which in turn flicked his right leg ahead of his body. He repeated the sequence of movements on his left side without pausing. There was labour involved but with the correct timing Brukup made his efforts look the opposite of cumbersome, more like a dance, one that called for the isolation of the various parts of the body precisely to show off their mobility and independence. This dance usually propelled him to his goal.

But Belinda's was crowded. Most of the clients, as Belinda dubbed the men who drank at the bar or played cards and dominoes before or after or in between seeing one of her many women in the several rooms upstairs, were inebriated to the point where their speech was abnormally loud, their gestures exaggerated. And if an instrument existed that could gauge their awareness of their immediate surroundings, it would have registered a negligible blip. Brukup cast the waitress a questioning glance.

'The Ministry of Defence.'

Brukup winced and rattled his head as if her words were insects that had unwittingly flown into his ear. 'We have a border war on our hands and the Ministry of Defence having a ball,' he muttered to himself.

He heard his name. Before he could turn his head to look back at the source, a heavy slap landed on his back. Brukup catapulted into a table. Cards, drinks and money flew. The men around the table sprang into various defensive moves to save their clothing, knocking over their chairs and cursing. Brukup crashed to the floor. His legs were splayed at improbable angles but his arms were in front of his face. Two of the men picked him up. They brushed at his clothing, asked him if he was all right and complained about their lost drinks and upset game. One of the men, who had remained seated throughout the commotion, was swiping at the air in front of him for his drink. Brukup stuffed a huge note into his hand. The man raised the note to his lips. The two who had helped Brukup to his feet grabbed the hand and wrestled the note from it. They thanked Brukup, straightened the table and chairs and kicked broken glass into a heap. One of the waitresses signalled with a dustpan and broom that the men could suspend their footballing skills for the evening. Brukup brushed his chest once and froze. Bits of glass he'd landed on had stuck to him. He peered down the broad bridge of his nose with one closed eye as if looking down the barrel of a rifle. There were several splinters sticking out at angles and making colourful prisms of the white bar light, but there was no blood.

'Brukup, darling!' Tracy shouted, throwing her sixteen stone at him. When she stepped back, Brukup looked her up and down. He felt a warm tingle coil its way through his groin. She was dressed in an extra-large man's shirt. Three buttons around the midriff were the only ones fastened. The shirt reached down to her considerable thighs. With the lower buttons undone it revealed flashes of her pubic hair whenever she moved. She apologised for slapping him on the back and before he could protest at her carelessness she took his hand, planted many moist kisses on it and led him towards a room to the left of the bar. The room belonged to the waitresses. Since Brukup could barely negotiate stairs it was known as Brukup's room by Belinda's special decree. Brukup urged Tracy to go ahead. He wouldn't be able to walk properly if she held his hand. As he watched her swaggering behind, he wished they were in the sea; then she could hold anything she wished and he'd still be able to do somersaults.

Brukup was rapid in settling himself on his back on the couch. Tracy unbuckled his trousers and pulled them to his ankles, slipped the three buttons of her shirt through their eyelets, shrugged the shirt off her shoulders and onto the floor, then climbed onto him.

'Easy now.'

'Don't I always, honey?'

'You are a wave, ride gently over me.'

'Yes, darling, let me use my tide to smooth your rocks.'

'Smooth them, my tidal wave, smooth them.'

Tracy dragged her hips backwards and forwards as she plucked the glass splinters from Brukup's chest. Brukup became tongue-tied. Soon his eyes crossed, his lids fluttered and closed and he sank weightlessly towards Atlantis.

An Ear to the Ground

'OPEN WIDE.'

We must win the countryside, by hook or by crook. The President had intended his remark to dampen the high spirits of his cabinet and advisers. He knew they had invested too much in the overseas initiative and in so doing had surrendered, in their carnival mood, all semblance of fighting a serious election campaign.

'Wider, Mr President.'

Brukup had informed him of the extravagant public display of wealth and merriment by generals and officials of the Defence Ministry at Belinda's. Gamediser too had furnished him with eyewitness accounts of government leaflets lying undistributed in warehouses or else dumped by the truckload on waste ground.

'Still, please.'

Instead of being hung in every available public space in the city, many posters had simply been handed to schoolchildren to use as protective and decorative covers for their exercise books. Children can't vote, the President had reminded his colleagues. Blank leaflets flung at people from government cars, jeeps, trucks and mopeds were an act of genius, he continued, if what was meant by it was that the people should write their own campaign promises since their wish was the government's command.

'Open wider, sir.'

Leaflets dropped from army helicopters over rice and cane fields, coconut groves and acres of bush would be read by the wildlife of the country, all of whom would trot, hop or crawl to the voting stations without fail on election morning to vote for the government. Thank you, gentlemen, for your erudition in these affairs of state. Your hunger for office is manifest.

'Upper left seven cavity.'

The President banned all future visits to Belinda's until the election was over and left the election strategy meeting to keep his dentist appointment.

'Cavity! What do you mean, cavity? Richmond, I pay you good, blasted money to avoid cavities, not to report them!'

Dentist Richmond retracted his probing instruments from the mouth just in time and maintained his steady downward gaze as it opened and closed. He looked after the mouths of the entire cabinet, high-ranking civil servants and military top brass. He'd learned not to try to shut up a politician.

'I beg your pardon, Mr President, I meant aperture. Using diamonds as fillings is a risk – you are lucky you swallowed it, you could have choked or bitten on it and chipped a tooth.'

'You find a new assistant?'

'None as good as the last one you poached from me. How she doing?'

'She's a fine campaign secretary for twenty-five and stunning-looking, but her pussy hang down to her knee from dropping pickney every year since she seventeen.'

'Where did you send her?'

'England. You can have her back after this general election.'

Dentist Richmond thought about the temporary filling he was charged with installing in the President's mouth and started to sweat in the air-conditioned surgery for the first time since leaving medical school. Since the President's last visit, when he had hijacked Richmond's beautiful and efficient assistant and converted her into a jet-setting campaign secretary, there had been an eventful interlude. At 3.05 a.m., in the middle of a busy week, the opposition leader had woken Richmond out of a deep sleep with a burst abscess. Richmond reprimanded the opposition leader for allowing such an advanced state of decay to occur to his mouth and questioned his suitability for the office of president of even this veritable republic if such personal neglect was symptomatic of his approach to the job. In the hours of treatment that followed, which had lasted the rest of the night and ended at midday when the empty stomachs of the two men were complaining so loudly they couldn't hear themselves speak, Dentist Richmond's re-education had taken place.

In reply to the admonition, the opposition leader had reminded the dentist that since the present government had taken control of the country no new dentists had been trained and that there existed one dentist for every twenty-five thousand souls in the land. The dentists, most of whom were Cuban, had simply abandoned their practices nation-wide and returned home when the President renounced what he called imported communism for a more home-grown free economy, a speech which qualified his government for loans from the World Bank and International Monetary Fund. And, by the way, what had become of those borrowed millions? It was he who'd passed a presidential decree limiting dentists to one filling per patient per visit when it emerged that perfectly healthy teeth were hollowed and filled with magnesium to increase dentists' piecemeal pay. This led to a rush abroad of the American- and British-trained dentists, leaving only the Cuban-trained nationals whose certificates would only be valid in Cuba.

Between the scrapings and rinsings, the injections and drillings, the stuffing of cavities and the polishing of crevices, the opposition leader had detailed cases of tooth decay in the countryside which made Dentist Richmond weep. Children driven into rabid states of distraction by toothaches until they would bite on the legs of furniture. Adults able to consume fluids only, tortured night and day by pustulating gums. Ironmongers posing as dentists with instruments used to reshoe a donkey, using these very implements to pull teeth in children and the old alike, all filled with red rum without distinction to insensibility, and many thereafter needing the overproof crutch to quell the daylong, nightlong pain caused by the irreparable damage inflicted on them. Teeth growing unchecked in all directions in children. Babies whose milk teeth refused to see the light of day, informed by heredity and their mothers telling them about the plight they faced, as they lay curled in the amniotic bath of the womb, were born with hardened gums that could crack walnuts and snap off a nipple.

The opposition leader had ended with this exhortation. Under my government, Dentist Richmond, I would not have you decorating the mouths of the elite. You would have an international research and training institute into all aspects of dentistry. You would lead this nation to the top of the World Health Organisation statistics of countries with the healthiest mouths. You would become an ineradicable part of our social history of upliftment because you would have helped this nation to face a crusty loaf once more without the terror of losing their teeth in it.

Dentist Richmond sweated and fought to control a fine tremor in his hands as he faced the opposition leader's opposite and more powerful number in the chair. The Seven Seas cod-liver-oil breath of the President stifled him. He examined the gap he'd tunnelled down to the root and sideways into two good teeth to accommodate the diamond now on its mile-long journey through the President's entrails. Perfect in its uncut state, it had been a gift from the chief of a native Indian tribe. The diamond arrived after the President gave the tribe five million hectares of the country's

impenetrable rainforests. This same region was now con-
tested by a neighbouring country as theirs and not the
President's to give away. The President had replied that they
would have to come and take it, averting a full-scale war
only because of the other side's consideration for the native
Indian tribes caught in the middle. The pea-sized listening
device placed in Dentist Richmond's palm by the opposition
leader with the parting words that this country's future was
in his hands would fit snugly in that gap.

'What's holding you up, Richmond? You sweating and
shaking, you feel sick?'

Dentist Richmond bolted to attention. He summoned all
his self-control, mopped his brow and took a big gulp of the
conditioned air. 'I have something to show you, Mr
President.' The resolve in his voice made the reclined
President raise himself onto his elbows. Dentist Richmond
turned and walked to a cabinet where he'd stored the minute
bugging mechanism. He would hand it to the President, who
would then have more than sufficient grounds to erase the
opposition with an irrefutable charge of treason and fulfil a
regularly nursed daydream. All previous attempts had
failed: the planting of bodies in the houses of members of the
opposition with the blood smeared on them as they slept; the
bribed photochromotypologists who testified under oath
that the opposition leader with a child of twelve in
compromising nudity was not an identical-looking model
and a child prostitute posing for a camera but genuine; the
substitution of marijuana for tobacco in cigarettes resealed
in their packs and given to the opposition, who were then
arrested the moment they lit them; all these had been
rebuffed by the excellent legal representation of the opposition, so that they emerged from the murkily lit courthouses
into the invariable sunlight with untarnished reputations
bolstered by new angelic coronas of public sympathy.

'This device will help you win the election before it's fought and bury the opposition for ever.'

'You know more than a dentist should know, Richmond. So, you still in touch with that former assistant of yours? Those overseas votes she's cooking up mustn't get out, you know that?'

Dentist Richmond's tongue did not form the words he'd instructed it to utter. He heard himself say something entirely different as his mind reeled backwards and forwards over the information the President had just inadvertently imparted to him.

'What cooked overseas votes, Mr President?'

The President nodded and smiled with approval. 'So show me this secret weapon that will help me win the election before it takes place.'

'It's a cap for your tooth. No foreign bodies, no toothache, no hindrance to your irresistible rhetoric.' Richmond waited for the President to make himself comfortable. 'Open wide, Mr President.'

He lowered the microscopic bug into the presidential mouth. There was some prodding and pushing as he fixed it firmly in its place and the skill for which Richmond had become known throughout the land became apparent: the President began to doze.

One mile offshore, the minimum distance from the land allotted by the government for all non-government-owned presses, on a large yacht converted to house printing machines with money collected in buckets rattled at markets up and down the land, a receiver was surrounded by the leader of the opposition and members of his shadow cabinet, including a stenographer and sound recordist. All listened with appalling concentration to the snores, then a crackly instruction to 'Rinse, Mr President', then fuzzy gargling. The final signal was clear of any static, confirming beyond dispute that it was indeed he who carried the bug and not some double-cross by Richmond. The offshore amplified sound of an explosion, which must have scared the gulls circling the yacht, was duly noted and recorded when the President produced what never failed him if he was satisfied – wind. Cheers cannonaded into the sea air.

The President's initial to his best athletes to 'whip Singh's ass' had resulted in a string of embarrassing defeats. Each inflicted a damaging knot to the government's dream of a smooth campaign since Singh was seen as a candidate on the opposing side, even though each time he was questioned about the election he always said, 'May the best man win,' in keeping with his vow to stay out of what he termed the 'crab barrel' of politics. Long before the Ariel bout the President had run out of men and other measures had been set in motion by Gamediser, the second of his 'two right-hand men' as he called them, always with a loud laugh at his one and only neologism. So far all had failed to check Singh's untrammelled progress of conquering the nation's wrestlers. Then came the President's order to 'make Singh an offer he can't refuse'. And just in case the unthinkable happened, namely a Singh defeat, there was always the overseas initiative. He knew he had lost the majority of the nation to the opposition. But that was never the issue. Not popular support, but outright victory.

The President phoned Dentist Richmond. 'Every now and then I getting a vibration from that damn tooth you filled.'

Richmond replied in unthinking obedience and honesty, 'It's, it's, it's fe-fe-feed-ba-ba-ba-back.' He was incapacitated by the fact that the President was nowhere near his equalising treatment chair, where he exercised total control over his stammer, his mind and his patient.

'I beg your pardon, Richmond?'

Richmond swept his sterile instruments off their standing tray. The stainless-steel scrapers and prodders with their delicate hooks and pointed ends crashed onto his marble surgery floor. He banged the receiver on his head. The phone cracked and gashed his skull.

'Richmond, you there?'

A warm, squiggly red line drew itself on his face. He swiped it with the back of his hand and looked at it. The sight of his own blood blocked his ears and banished the clutch of confusing thoughts in his head, all except for one which shone brilliant and clear.

'Richmond!'

'Yes, Mr President.'

'What do you mean by feedback?'

'Acids, sir.'

'Acids?'

'Acids from the digestive tract, sir, stimulated by eating, have probably permeated to the root, causing the minor irritation registered in your brain as a vibration. Sir, it will stop very soon.'

'How soon, damn it?'

'Within the hour.'

'It had better, Richmond, or I'll tear the thing out myself.'

'Oh, you mustn't do that, sir.'

'Shoddy work, if you ask me, Richmond, shoddy work.'

Richmond apologised to the high, even tone of a vacant line. He sank exhausted into his treatment chair. A moment later he grabbed the phone. He didn't care if the opposition leader was in midstream – get him on the line. Was the opposition leader trying to commit suicide and take a trusting dentist along with him?

'Dr Richmond, I will be there immediately for my results.'

Again Richmond found himself complaining to a tone. He gathered his instruments on a tray, examined a couple and saw they had been damaged, and threw the lot into a dustbin. He cleaned up his cut head, washed his face and put on a clean pair of white overalls. He dialled his secretary and told her to cancel all his appointments and to ring his assistant and tell her to take the morning off. 'When the opposition leader arrives, bring him straight in.'

Dentist Richmond declined the proffered hand of the opposition leader by keeping his arms firmly buried in his pockets. The range had to be adjusted. New legislation had forced the yacht another mile out to sea. As a result, transport costs from the land and back had doubled. 'What you have done, Richmond, will earn you the highest merit in the land.'

Richmond stopped listening. He wondered what had taken the place of a knighthood when this former colony became independent, then a socialist republic. And now . . . now he didn't know what it had become or what high honour it could confer on him. He dug his hands out of his pockets and returned the embrace that caught him by surprise.

Gamediser

GAMEDISER HEAVED HIS right leg, then his left, then, using his fleshy fingers to grip the doorframe, his entire bulk out of the country's only Pontiac. The car's suspension bounced from a slope to its permanent lean towards the driver's side damaged by the sustained punishment of shouldering Gamediser. He stopped at Ariel ostensibly for a drink. Children and adults minding their stalls in the market square gathered to inspect the country's only Pontiac, allowed in against stringent import controls; without the slightest trace of inhibition, they stared at the body it had to convey, the heaviest person on the presidential payroll.

In confirmation of his grand-piano proportions Gamediser was also one of the President's least dispensable assets, second only to Brukup, with whom he shared the same height, five foot five inches, and a mutual dislike. Gamediser hated even to think about Brukup; it put him off his food. Since he was always about to eat or concluding a meal or in pursuit of a meal, virtually no room was left in his thoughts (on a conscious level) for Brukup. He hated Brukup's frugal nature: riding a bicycle when he should be in something big, bright and imported. This abstinence presumably ran in the man's very demeanour: his thin legs, narrow bicycle, sparse vocabulary and needling eyes that pierced everything they hit, yet managed never to rest on anything for more than a moment. Gamediser knew that these very qualities made Brukup the President's right-hand man and relegated him to a permanent second place since he could never hope to emulate them. His eyes did not alight on things fleetingly, they landed squarely on them and consumed them. He did not speak in hushed tones, nor find the smallest number of words that would capture precisely what he wanted to say. Voluble and loud, he flavoured everything with copious amounts of description.

Gamediser had grown accustomed to stopping traffic or silencing a market when he appeared. They could look as much as they liked as long as they did not touch. He had stickers on his car that read, 'Look but don't touch.' He elbowed the revolver strapped near his armpit, more as a comfort to himself than a threat to his audience. To banish the last scrap of doubt about his own inadequacy, Gamediser targeted an empty can, pivoted twenty-eight stone on one foot, swung his Italian alligator shoe and pitched the can several yards. The silent market exploded. Gamediser raised his eyebrows. Those who did not see his goalkeeper's clearing of the ball from the goal mouth to way beyond the halfway line, asked and were told and they renewed the laughter. This drew more people who had to be informed and who in turn added to its long duration. Gamediser allowed his revolver to be seen by stretching his arms above his head so that his jacket opened. The laughter fizzled out. He bowed. Applause followed.

He approached a drinks stall and paid for two glasses of mauby, pausing only to put down his first empty glass and turn the second full one upwards in his face. The cold drink tunnelled deep into his exceptional bulk. He pulled a handkerchief from his back trouser pocket with such swiftness that people nearby took a few cautionary steps away. He dabbed his lips, then unfolded the cloth with a flick and mopped his brow. As he folded and replaced it in his back pocket, he asked those closest to him if one of them could point out the house where the brave soul resided whom the magnificent Singh would no doubt reduce from a proud opponent to a bundle of shame. Everyone looked puzzled. He asked if this was indeed Ariel, Cooperative Republic village number ——. Everyone nodded. Again he described Singh the ungovernable converting good citizens to useless pieces of sculpture. Again puzzled looks greeted him. 'Where does Singh's challenger live?' Recognition flooded everyone's face. Gamediser buried the disdain for these people that flowered in his eyes and in the corners of his mouth and planted a false smile in its place.

'I live with him, sir,' Red Head volunteered. He appeared to be saluting as he shaded his eyes from the sun.

'No need to salute, I'm not an army man.' Gamediser's smile broadened. The child kept his open hand to his forehead. 'Ride with me in my car to this place.' Gamediser projected what he estimated to be his trustworthy daddy smile.

'No. You drive. I going walk.'

Red Head set off in a fast walk followed by a significant portion of the crowd, who abandoned their shopping or got someone to guard the produce on their stalls. Gamediser wanted to call out to him but decided he'd play along with the child. The Pontiac that was almost level when empty creaked and sloped towards the driver's seat as Gamediser slumped into it. He pushed the key home, turned on the ignition and sat still to catch his breath and bask in the air conditioning. The cool he'd felt inside from his two long drinks became exteriorised and played around his neck, chest and arms, fanning beads of sweat. The beads would join into a necklace, then break and disappear down his shirt front. New beads would again form around his neck, thread themselves and break once more. Whereas his handkerchief only served to delay the process, the air conditioning in his Pontiac curtailed it.

Gamediser peered into the wavering heat that liquidised the floating birds and elasticated the trunks of trees and people. It melted to invisibility the child who was meant to guide him to Singh's arena. He accelerated and switched on the wipers and wash on his windscreen, clearing it of red dust and the stubborn stuff of squashed insects. Switching the wipers off, he leaned over the steering wheel to improve his view. Still nothing. He stopped, and hit the dashboard with his open hand. 'Impudent little scunt!' He was contemplating reversing to the market and asking for directions again or simply driving back to the capital when the child's figure trembled out of the heat and solidified next to the Pontiac.

'You coming or you going?'

'Hop in, hop in!'

Though jovial, Gamediser was insistent. As Red Head climbed into the front seat, Bash Man Goady appeared beside him followed by three cousins and Sten.

'Who are all these people?'

'Family.'

Sten climbed in next to Red Head. The others filed into the back after Bash Man Goady finished arranging a sheet on the seat Gamediser had pointed out to him and instructed him to spread. The children tried to see what made them shiver when moments ago they had been baking in the sun. They showed each other the goose pimples on their arms and named the trees they passed and houses they recognised and their school. Gamediser took his time lighting his pipe. He sucked audibly on it. Puffs of smoke met the roof of the car and evened out as if poured there. The children inhaled its perfume. Gamediser bit gently on his pipe as he explained the air-conditioning system. Each word was a wisp of smoke; the end of each sentence, a puff. The pattern was such that if the children in the back seat were deaf and unable to read his lips they could at least understand him through his smoke signals.

Wheels passed the car, sprinting as he always did on the

home stretch. The children shouted his name but the car windows were closed. Gamediser raised his eyebrows, looked at the cyclist, then at the speedometer, then again at the cyclist.

'He's flying!'

'That Uncle Wheels. He going win the National Cycle Championships.' Red Head wriggled himself higher in the seat.

'I better follow him then.' Gamediser accelerated.

'Our uncle Bounce going beat Singh,' Bash Man Goady boasted.

'What! He's an uncle too?'

'All we uncles and aunts can do something.' Red Head wanted to boast about Footsy's water-bearing capability but was censored when he glanced over his shoulder at his older brother, who shot him a stern look.

When Gamediser's 'I would consider it an honour to meet these two geniuses' met with silence as if he'd switched to explaining how the atom is split, he rephrased it. 'I can't wait to meet them.'

'Is the next house on the right.' Sten pointed ahead.

'I play draughts.'

'Are you any good?'

'Good? Good! My brother don't lose a game since we mother went away.' Bash Man Goady nodded to emphasise his words and all the children hissed their assent.

'And how long has that been?'

'Five months, two weeks and five days.'

'So you've won against all your friends?'

'I don't play children.'

Gamediser looked at the child in the seat beside him. 'You heard about our National Draughts Championships?'

'Yes.'

'Perhaps you can win that.'

To sprint, Wheels raised himself off the saddle and

crouched forward on the handlebars, throwing the bike from left to right. Then he sat upright, his hands off the handlebars, no longer pedalling, and let the bike cruise the last few yards to the front gate. The Pontiac crept up on him soundlessly, whipping up further volumes of dust to add to the library already raised by Wheels. Wheels stopped at the log bridge to carry his bike over it. Dust from the Pontiac made him look back. Red Head, Bash Man Goady, Sten and the others poured out of the side of the car nearest the trench. Gamediser prised himself upwards. The suspension made its usual protests. The children ran and hugged Wheels. They all spoke.

'We doing forty-five and you fly past!'

'Only forty-five?' Wheels mocked.

Gamediser held out his right arm towards Wheels and smiled from yards away. He closed the yards between them with a walk that was more like the motion of an armoured tank with a steering problem, not quite able to travel forwards without twisting this way and that. Before Wheels could finish drying his sweaty palm on his sweatshirt and take the outstretched hand of Gamediser, Grandad intervened.

'You are not welcomed in my house. Say what you have to say right here.'

The children froze. Wheels straightened and ordered them across the log bridge into the yard. Granny, Footsy, Beanstalk and Bounce stood their ground behind Grandad.

Gamediser hovered on the spot. 'Let's be civilised about this. The sun beating down overhead.'

But Grandad interrupted him, 'I don't care if the sun in your top pocket. If civilised defines your party's conduct in this election campaign, you can keep it.'

Gamediser smiled. He wanted dearly to draw his revolver and let it answer for him. He felt sweat sprout and become beaded on his forehead. He ran his index finger across it and flicked off the water. The old man's words had sounded too much like his own. They left him surprised and floundering. He thought about his revolver. He glanced up the road and saw a small crowd approaching. The old man and his people were already back in their yard. Gamediser wondered why that talented fool carried his bicycle on his shoulders and which of the other two might be the bait for Singh to gobble up. The tall one was Singh's height but he was stringy. The short one had a prominent head on his shoulders and Brukup's piercing eyes but he looked like a boy. Gamediser waved them away and glided uncertainly back to his car. He skidded away, raising what seemed like his own weight in dust.

'Stay in the capital where you belong!' Grandad shouted at the dust cloud as it drifted and painted the leaves of roadside trees with yet another coat. Some of the cloud climbed another rung on its tall painter's ladder and stretched with its unwelcome brush towards the houses set back from the road.

'We should have fed Gamediser to Bubble Back.'

'That would have set up Bubble Back with food for the year!'

Gamediser drove straight from Ariel to Belinda's. He always visited Belinda's when angry. He snarled, grateful for the unexpected rebuttal from the old man at Ariel. The idea had crossed his mind when he woke at 6 a.m. with a surprise erection. But it withered away seconds after he had peed. He had made up his mind to contrive a quarrel with someone some time that day to procure a session at Belinda's. In the past when he had gone there cold, expecting to be put on some fire and brought to the boil, the girl had to labour hard and long to get even a flicker of warmth from him. She would take his little dead meat, as he called it, into her mouth, switch to milking it with both hands heavily lubricated, sit on it and rodeo until she was out of breath and

117

bored, tie him up and beat him until he got scared and wept and eventually released the tiny, unhemmed white flag that signalled his surrender.

He hit on the anger solution thanks to Brukup. One evening they had both turned up at Belinda's, each demanding to have Tracy before the other. Gamediser became so infuriated he huffed and puffed. When he saw all the eyes in the bar trained on his crotch he looked down and saw the miracle tenting his trousers. He fancied it was a truncheon raised by sheer willpower in order to club Brukup to pieces. Brukup conceded Gamediser's need was the greater of the two and stepped aside.

Gamediser pulled into Belinda's yard and found her on the veranda fanning herself languidly. She had her feet up. A tall glass sweated with some cold, sweet drink. She eyed the Pontiac from boot to bonnet with thinly veiled hostility. As it spilled its contents, she shouted, 'What time you call this, man? My girls need to rest. They work all night. Come back later.'

Gamediser did not bother to respond until he was less than three feet from her. He pointed to his tented trousers. 'You see this, it don't wait for no woman.'

Belinda was unrelenting. 'Man, the girls need their rest.'

'Belinda, how long you know me? How often do I come knocking at your door at an unsociable hour? Send me away now and I don't know when the call will reach me again.'

She got up angrily and went inside. He followed her. The bar was hotter than the veranda. A ceiling fan spun uselessly. Belinda went behind the bar and fixed Gamediser two huge drinks. She put ice in the glass until it spilled. Gamediser smiled.

'I want Tina.'

'Have Tracy instead.'

'No, Tina.'

'But the girl had a hard night.'

'I'll pay double.'

'Double?'

'Double.'

'Man, your need must be great.'

Belinda shouted up the stairs for Tina. A tall, thin girl with matted shoulder-length hair appeared at the top of the stairs rubbing the sleep from her eyes.

'Girl, I sorry to wake you. See to this customer. He paying double.'

Tina wanted to complain but she could use the extra money. She looked at Gamediser sulkily, betraying her fifteen years. She picked up his two drinks and dragged her feet into the back room. Gamediser winked at Belinda, slapped five big bills into her hand and followed Tina.

Belinda shook her head in dismay at Gamediser's back. When he turned sideways to get through the door, she suppressed a laugh. Resuming her feet-up vigil on the veranda, she changed the left, right action of her automatic fanning to shoo the children from the polished, lopsided, red Pontiac that had drawn them out of the shade from their games. She heard a girl crying and thought the whimpering came from inside her bar. Impossible. She rattled her head to rid it of the notion. Only women were allowed in this establishment.

Disappearances

THE CAPITAL WOKE early on election morning. Leaflets blew along the streets, tired of their slogans and in search of a bed. Engines shuddered to life, shaking off the night's dew clinging to bonnets and bumpers. Light above the city appeared to peel back layer after layer of these grey blankets to reveal white linen sheets on a dishevelled bed.

The President rose before his allotted 5 a.m. call for his twice-weekly beach ride, 'come rain or shine', shaved, showered and slapped a guava-scented perfume on his face. Still naked, he stood before a full-length mirror and thumped his chest several times, muttering, 'President, President.' Two personal assistants entered and helped his naked frame into a string vest and cotton shirt, no underpants (he found them constricting: 'Can't breathe, can't think'), then a purple uniform whose many medals chimed during the fitting and brushing, and quietened after the last brushstroke banished unseen specks of dust from shoulders, chest and lapels.

Queues had already formed at the makeshift polling stations. Soldiers, posted there the night before, woke to see quietly spoken citizens, from street sweepers to stockbrokers, lining the streets and shuffling around on tiptoe in an effort not to disturb the sleep of their venerable protectors. Some of the city's cockerels, confused by this activity, did not bother to crow. Instead, they chose to look on, perhaps feeling sidelined by this city, awake before its time and in an unspeaking, serious way going about its inscrutable intent, as if the day had always begun with the activity of mid-morning.

At a ramshackle but no less famous Great House, the leader of the opposition and his wife opened their eyes and smiled. She told him this was his last day as opposition leader. He told her that this time tomorrow she would be his First Lady; that is, officially, since she had always been his first and only lady. An old cook's early tinkering in the kitchen had served as an alarm. The opposition leader's and his wife's mouths watered as the cook's fried plantain and pepperpot subsumed all of the house's two hundred years of fragrances.

Barrels of indelible ink waited to receive the sponges of the nation's thumbs, not to incorporate the illiterate in the democratic process (according to the official records, in this republic, everyone was literate) but to prevent fraud. The radio stations played calypsos about Democracy and General Election: two famous characters lionised in rhythm and raucous rhyme. Overseas observers patrolled the polling booths, checked the padlocks on ballot boxes or else randomly ran their eyes down voting registers to ensure that names did not exist in duplicate or triplicate. The first rays of the sun varnished the capital to perfection.

The President paraded in purple, on an imaginary horse, before the full-length mirror. His two assistants stood out of the way of his sudden swivels as he changed direction, his side kicks that spurred him on, and his rabbit punches denoting difficulty with the reins. They described outside as if they were one voice. 'Sky blue, sun just start, air cool, ground damp with dew, fowl cock crow long time or not at all, tide low, but salt blasting the air bad as ever, far-off cloud reach here by midday, sun bound to get hot, hot, palace bread still baking, milk not deliver yet . . .'

'Shut up before I knock out your false teeth,' the President interjected. Having knocked out the real ones long ago, he'd

121

paid for the cost of some false sets and had taken to dashing them from his assistants' mouths at the slightest provocation, with knuckles hidden behind precious stones. He was always a little jittery around the time of his early-morning rides, though he enjoyed them once they got under way. His assistants felt this nervousness and emulated it.

The drive from the palace to the private beach was quick and unfussy: a three-mile stretch of private road through a residential area populated by millionaire businessmen, high-ranking civil servants and government ministers, with guards at the gates who saluted when the President's procession passed them; vehicles containing four horses and two grooms, six armed bodyguards, a secretary and his special guest of the night before, who was joining him on the ride. At a bend in the road where there were no trees, the sun splashed its sharp light into the President's eager face thrust out of the bulletproof limousine window, causing him to draw his head into the vehicle and swear. On the straight section of the road, with the sun at the side of him and a protective lining of trees, he stuck his head out again and enjoyed the breeze whipping tears from his eyes, giving him a taste of the imminent ride.

The President's restless stallion and his friend's more amenable mare were shadowed at a respectful distance by two mounted bodyguards. Three others accompanied by a groom followed in a beach buggy which retreated even further to minimise the impact of engine noise on the President's dawn reverie. A second groom and the last of the bodyguards remained with the vehicles. At one point the President's stallion and his friend's mare emerged riderless from behind a sand dune. The two mounted bodyguards galloped to their President's aid, guns drawn, only to come upon a different riding scene: their President astride his night-long frolic, riding her as if she were a mare and using his whip liberally on her behind and legs. Both guards withdrew at double speed and signalled frantically to the beach buggy, which was approaching fast, with poised automatic weapons, to stay back. The driver swerved, but too sharply, and the jeep overturned, spilling its contents. There was much loud swearing as they brushed themselves clean of sand and joined forces to return the jeep onto its wheels. The two mounted guards chased the President's edgy stallion and his friend's calm mare. A dishevelled President walked clear of the dunes with his companion trailing behind him.

'What's all the commotion?'

Explanations were offered out of the reach of the President's bejewelled left jab.

As soon as the President was installed in his saddle, the stallion reared onto its hind legs. 'The scunt is trying to throw me!' He bawled and dug his spurred heels into the animal's hind quarters. He tugged on the reins as if to feed the bit down its throat and almost succeeded in throwing the horse onto its back.

The two mounted guards shouted advice and tried to grab the reins while fighting to control their horses. They were joined by the three guards from the upturned jeep and the groom, arms waving and all firing instructions. The stallion reared and then kicked its hind legs, shook its mane and whinnied like a mimic of the men surrounding it.

'Fuck off, you baboons!'

His men fell silent and backed away. This calmed the stallion to the extent that it no longer reared and kicked, but it kept shaking its mane and pawing at its ears as if its crown of hair was somehow detachable. The groom grabbed the reins and helped the President to dismount. Then he peered into the horse's ears and spoke, which seemed to have an immediate calming effect. The groom turned to speak to the President but he had retreated several yards off and was receiving a cuddle from his girlfriend which involved the usual embrace supplemented by bouts of running her hands up and down his back and thighs. Instead of looking at the President as he spoke, the groom addressed the surrounding beach, dunes and surf.

'There's nothing wrong with this horse. He might be hearing something we can't. Some high frequency perhaps.'

The President ducked and his bodyguards formed a ring around him and his girlfriend. She gripped his arms and started to whimper and pray. He shrugged her off. She fell into the arms of the bodyguard nearest to her and he lowered her gently onto the sand, then resumed his alert stance.

'What do you mean by frequency?' the President shouted, still crouching.

'I'm not sure. Some sort of transmitter.'

The opposition leader's night-duty radiographer could not believe his ears. His 'Oh, scunt! Trouble!' poisoned the carnival air on the floating headquarters. All night he'd monitored the President's admonishments to his newly acquired companion, ranging from 'You sharpen your teeth with a file?' to 'Is not chewing gum you eating, girl!', followed by his snoring and occasional commands to women in the phases of his erect penile sleep to 'Bend over' and 'Take that and that.'

The opposition leader's special breakfast, during which he indulged his favourite daydream of riding a six-horse stagecoach called the Nation across arid savannah fringed by impenetrable rainforest, was destroyed by the news of the President's almost-discovered listening device. The driver of the stagecoach (a part the opposition leader had cast himself in) toppled in a forward somersault from his high perch and landed under the very hooves meant to propel him and the Nation to some future destination. He began to sweat. The last time perspiration covered him so entirely he was smelling the barrel of a revolver thrust into his nose by the interior minister during a parliamentary debate in which he'd questioned 'the minister's use of the road-making machine – on hire from the United States at enormous expense to the nation – and part of the road gang, whose honest wages were paid for by the taxpayer, over a weekend, to dig a garden swimming pool and build a U-shaped drive leading in one gate up to the said minister's front door and out another'.

The President tapped his pockets and looked at his decorated chest as if he half expected to identify a transmitter among the mixed metals, some precious, of his medals. He eyed the groom and his bodyguards from head to toe, then turned his attention to the stallion. His face took on the impassive stare an executioner reserves for his next victim. The groom saw his President's blank eyes, tight-set lips and rapidly compressing jaws. Right away, he unharnessed the stallion of bridle, saddle and blanket, which the horse obediently allowed with little movement, letting the bit fall from its mouth and shivering a little in the early-morning sea breeze. When the President approached the stallion, it reared and recoiled, baring its teeth and snorting. By the vigorous shaking of its mane, it was possible to believe a wasp's nest had been disturbed between its ears.

'It's you, Mr President, you must be bugged!' The groom hugged the neck of the stallion to calm it.

'Impossible!'

The President's face creased and his eyes widened. He began to circle his bodyguards, groom and mistress in wide steps. The last time he had walked like that he had just swallowed his diamond filling and was about to fire a handgun at his chef for daring to serve a tough steak to him when he was reminded that it wouldn't look good in the presence of a delegation from the International Monetary Fund.

'Take off your clothes!' He shot a cold look at his shuddering mistress. 'All of you!' Something was wrong, meaning, everyone, except for him, was culpable.

At the floating headquarters of the opposition leader, jewellery, keys and loose change were heard tumbling into the sand. The President instructed his groom to bury everything. He grew impatient watching and began to help. His bodyguards kept one hand over their crotches and the other on their guns and shivered and stamped the beach for warmth like the stallion. His mistress folded herself into a ball, hugged her knees and rocked.

'Get your hands off your lazy balls and help me bury these things!'

Once the clothes were all gone, the President again approached the stallion. Again it reared and retreated. He swore at the animal, balefully surveyed his groom, bodyguards and infantile mistress and peeled off the presidential raiments while the stallion looked on calmly from a safe distance. Naked, he walked with big strides towards the horse but it whinnied, reared and retreated from him.

The opposition leader, conveyed by speedboat from his home to his offshore headquarters with the thought that he was now technically away from his country on the day of an election he was certain to win (a day when any other leader in any other sovereign state would have been in the bosom of his country, safely ensconced among his supporters in the capital), steadied himself on two colleagues as the horse whinnied out of the transistor. In his dream the six horses whinnied for joy as they galloped harnessed to the Nation and he cracked a celebratory whip in the speeding air above their heads. There was none of the panic broadcasted in this stallion's cry. A loud presidential curse followed.

'Mad, blasted, mother-fucking, dumb beast! There's nothing on me!'

He grabbed a handgun from the nearest naked, gun-brandishing body, and shoved it out of the way with a slap to the chest. The body toppled into the sand, flat on its back, when it united the hand robbed of its gun with the other hand already cupping genitalia, instead of using one or both of them to break its fall. A mixture of presidential curses and rapidly discharged bullets brought the stallion to its front knees and neck, then onto its side, where it twitched as its life oozed from several little openings. The President flung the empty gun at the horse. He dragged his mistress to her feet and pushed her into the jeep, jumped behind the wheel and sped off towards his limousine.

The groom's 'This horse is more human than most humans' got drowned in the surf and sea breeze, judged equally responsible for the water swept from his eyes. He grabbed a gun from the bodyguard nearest to him, causing the others to train their weapons on him, but he ignored them and knelt beside the stallion, whose limbs jerked periodically as if it were having a dream. A single gun report stilled the horse and started the groom muttering. 'My baby, my baby, my baby.' The bodyguards dug up the clothes, shook sand from their trousers, pulled them on and ran after the President.

'Get Dentist Richmond on the phone. That thing has to be removed from his mouth before we all end up dead.'

The opposition leader also called for a clean suit, peeling off his drenched election suit, a grey Savile Row, shaking his head to clear the gunshots that had dethroned the stage-coach driver of his dreams.

'Get Richmond on the phone! How many times do I have to ask? Open a few windows, this place stinks. Talk about preparing for government; not one of you can manage a little personal hygiene, farting quietly and whistling like is nothing. Is antisocial!' His handful of loyal volunteers who

had not slept for days feigned alertness by striding purpose-
fully in various directions.

'Dentist Richmond on the line, sir.'

'Oh, good morning, Richmond.'

'Don't you good morning me. What time do you call this?'

'All right, go back to sleep and wait for the President to
call on you himself and demand an explanation about the
smart piece of dentistry you performed for him.'

Dentist Richmond began to bawl, barely managing to get
out a few curses. 'Stink-mouth! Boasting about a new
nation. Hot air I should never have heeded. Ruined!'

'Not ruined, Richmond, dead, unless you collect yourself.'

'Kiss my ass! You turn up here with an abscess big as a
latrine pit and you want my respect! Shit-face!'

'Richmond, pull yourself together! Don't let this thing slip
out of our hands. Not now.'

There was a long pause when the dentist's whimpering
could be heard above his struggle to bring his breathing
under control.

'I'm sorry sir, it's early, you scared me. You're right. There
is no better alternative to this country than you. I will do my
best.'

'Thank you, Richmond. You are the best.'

'Thank you, sir.'

The opposition leader held the dead tone to his ear for a
while, wiped the salt dripping from his forehead into his eyes
and called for his change of clothes before 'next week'. His
laundry assistant, who was also his personal secretary and
wife, held up a clean shirt for him to fill as she muttered
something about how the closer he got to the presidency, the
more pungent his sweat became.

III

Homing

Directory Enquiries

HER GOVERNMENT'S OBLIQUE election strategy felt like a personal insult. A senior campaign secretary should not be five thousand miles away from home. Print-blackened fingers had combed thousands of pages of telephone directories for names and addresses to add to her growing list of nationals of voting age resident in England. This was a game to preoccupy a child. Her two eldest children, whom she missed, played one similar to it when they idled away the odd afternoon by the roadside recording the number plates of vehicles. At least they got valuable practice at improving their writing. All she had were dirty, aching fingers and eye strain from reading vast quantities of close print. She also had three disgruntled young children under her feet.

She knew she had to invent a few Johnsons and Simonses. Her work would be checked by the embassy for what it called 'credulity' before being sent to her government. If the embassy staff detected one entry that had a bogus feel to it, they could mar her standing. Yet she was supposed to insert fabricated names and addresses on her list of overseas votes. Nobody cares! Yes, they do! They care to catch someone out and bring them down in order to promote themselves. This debate with herself was the kind of thing that would keep her from climbing up the government ranks. Her conscience was too developed for her own good. It slowed her down and made her look like a worker who was diligent, efficient and reliable, but one who lacked initiative, because the first three attributes, when taken together, amounted to an encumbrance of the fourth. And the fourth was the most valuable human asset to a government during an election that all the analysts and polls said was likely to put it out of office. Her job was straightforward: quadruple, by any means necessary, the list of names of voters living in England who were sympathetic to the government. She was sure her counterparts in New York, Miami, Washington and Toronto, charged with the same brief, had probably accomplished their targets and were using the extra time and money to shop, nightclub and sightsee. Not her. She had run out of money with half the list to complete. And she had moved from the salubrious avenues of Kensington to a slum in east London, giving up a high-ceilinged two-bedroom flat with a view of the park for two downstairs rooms in someone's mildewed house.

The clause 'any means' liberated her from her moral bind. She had permission to be creative at the expense of her inveterate honesty. So it came to pass that when she found a Johnson in Brixton she would try and locate another not too far away in south London just to create the impression that the two were close relatives. With a Simons she'd employ the reverse tactic, putting two of them at opposite ends of the city. This complicated her task somewhat since she had to find two Simonses, one in Bromley, the other in Crouch End. In the case of the Johnsons she actually caught a number 38 red double-decker bus from Victoria station to the Brixton address and checked if the second Johnson was within reasonable walking distance of the first. The children loved these rides on what they called 'the Big Red Vroom Vroom'. Their incessant questions about their absent brothers and father ceased. She could do without questions to which she had no answers as she had done (so far) without their reprobate father. But what would she do if he turned up tomorrow? Order him to take off his clothes or scream at him until he disappeared once more? She didn't know for sure. The two boys were another matter. She would try everything to bring them to her or get her back to them.

Before long she had to abandon her scrupulous tactics, which squandered too much of her valuable time, and revert to the more remote technique of reading road maps, letting her fingers walk on her behalf. Most of her time was eaten up with estimating the walking time between two addresses from the distances given on the scale, or else finding a second matching name and an address poles apart from the first. She tried to involve her three bored children by getting them to identify the metrical foot of a name. Metre was the only thing she believed her father had ever taught her that was worth remembering. Johnson is a trochee, she'd make them repeat after her. Then they'd say it along with her. Jones is a – she wouldn't say what Jones was, stopping in mid-flow to test whether they really knew the answer or were reading her lips. When that bored her she got them to calculate the distance between two addresses by measuring a mile as one joint on a finger. She'd ask them, if they had five joints, how many miles did they have, and then get the youngest to count out five joints on two fingers. If he couldn't do it she'd pass it on to the second youngest. The eldest of the three would sometimes shout the answer if he lost patience waiting for his turn. And since he rarely got a turn he acted as her assistant by ensuring his youngest brother did not miss a joint on a finger. But the game was scuppered once the youngest worked out that the number of joints was always equivalent to the number of miles and he started shouting the answer when she'd said only the first part of the question.

Her weekend trips to Birmingham, Liverpool and Manchester were curtailed too. The boys had looked forward to those weekends and had been willing to suspend all their demands during the week. They'd become used to hearing

that there would be no train this weekend if they misbe-
haved. The journeys were passed by seating two of them
with their backs to the destination and the third seated
opposite looking at the approaching scenery. He would
name something that was coming up and they would try and
identify its colour as they flew backwards from it. Or he'd
say the colour and they'd identify something with that
colour. Even this game had its complications. If he said
green, the options of what would be green out in the middle
of the English countryside were unlimited. The cleverer of
the two brothers sitting with their backs to the scenery
would guess tree or grass before either could properly be
seen. If a colour was called and there were two things
bearing that colour, the one who named the most numerous
thing won that round. Sometimes the campaign secretary
would have to abandon her list or knitting to mediate a
dispute. But if she decided that black must belong to cows,
not pigs, since cows are generally more numerous than pigs,
but it was a pig farm that they'd passed, she'd make the loser
cry over the injustice done to him by her decision. Then she'd
call a halt to the game and the children would fidget and
gradually resume a silent version of it. This involved huge
mouthings of words and sudden gushes of air as they raced
to answer silently, until she'd laugh, shake her head, tell
them that they must have been sent to her as her trials and
crosses on this earth, and make them promise not to have
any disputes or she'd scrap it again. Then she'd act as a
starting gun for them by shouting 'play'. This would get her
looking at the English countryside. These skies were too
close to the ground. On a cloudy day, when the front of the
train could be seen as it curved round a hill, its roof appeared
to shave the lowered heads of the cloud.

The money shortage meant trips on the Big Red Vroom
Vrooms were fewer too. This state of impecuniousness
made the children more of a burden than ever. They asked

her daily when they were leaving for home. They asked how their two elder brothers were coping without them and her. They fought among themselves frequently, and, whereas in the past, a stern look or harsh word had proved sufficient to check any recalcitrant behaviour, now she found herself having to prise them apart and put herself between them to stop them from exchanging blows. One time the biggest had even kicked his younger brother through her legs after she'd separated them, driving her so mad she'd slapped him across his face and seen her hand print blossom there. She counted the six-and-a-half hours it took to sink out of sight.

The deterioration in their behaviour did more than anything to convert her from a zealot for procedure into a creative deployer of initiative. She had to complete her assignment before her children starved to death or murdered each other. There was an outside chance that she might murder one of them. They made her lose her temper several times every day. She'd leave them to watch television in the living room that doubled as a dining room and trebled as a playroom too while she worked on the double bed that filled the second room. The two rooms were divided by a curtain. Noise from the television in the living room had to be kept to a minimum to enable her to work in the bedroom. The boys sat so close to it that their feet rested on the television stand. They were five, four and three years old. Every morning they got up, put the television on, listened to the even tone or, if they were lucky, organ music, and waited for the first programme to be broadcast. One of them would turn the brightness up or down as if the test card clown had walked into a tropical midday sun or out into the thickness of night. They'd try and guess what colours the various shades of grey in the picture represented. The deep shade on the skull made the clown's hair red or green or blue. But if the dark, round nose was red, then it had to be green or blue hair since that shade was deeper. She interrupted them by ordering them to sit further away from the screen, otherwise they would be blinded and their brains would shrivel up and rattle around in their heads. Each was handed a bowl which he placed on the floor between his feet. Then they took turns to fill their bowls with cereal and cover it with tablespoons of white sugar. After that delicate task of sprinkling the sugar as evenly as possible they'd wait for her to pour hot milk over it. The eldest loved the skin on the top of the boiled milk, the youngest hated it, the middle one didn't mind either way, but the campaign secretary would spoon the skin off with her index finger on her way from the kitchen she shared with the couple who owned the house because if milk could be made as thick and as sweet as the skin that forms whenever she boiled the milk, that was all she'd eat. She also placed glasses of concentrated orange juice diluted with hot water on the floor, surveyed the scene, then went back to work. The boys would immediately inch themselves forwards to their original places in front of the television.

Her list was kept in a cardboard box under the bed. If she went out of the house, the first thing she did when she returned was get on her knees, thrust her hand in the dark, pull out the box, look to see if it had been tampered with in any way, and push it back into the dark. Then she would take off her coat and make sure the front door was closed and all her children were inside. Her urgent need to complete the list, in particular that portion of it pertaining to Birmingham, Manchester and Liverpool, made her rely on maps without recourse to the directories of those cities. She picked streets and populated them with invented names and house numbers. A name was made up by simply switching around another name from a different city or adding a letter to it. Robert Charles in London became Charles Roberts in Manchester. She was certain Robert was an iamb but wondered if Charles was a spondee.

When at last the number of names on her list matched the

miles she'd been removed from her beloved republic, she knew her labour was nearing its conclusion. This was her signal to make that collect call to South America. 'Children, put on your coats, we're going to the phone box.'

The boys watched Tom as he ran into Jerry's brick-wall trap and took on the flat shape of the wall, complete with the individual brick markings. Tom fell like a playing card to the floor, then zapped back to his old self before resuming his pursuit of Jerry. She went to the television and switched it off. The boys howled.

'I said we're going out, now get your coats.'

All she said down the mouthpiece was, 'The constituency is complete,' and hung up. Her second call was to the embassy.

'The constituency is complete.'

This time she did not hang up. She was told to bring the list to the embassy at her earliest convenience. She asked for an increase in her allowance. The voice in the earpiece sighed in thinly disguised exasperation and reminded her that she'd gone way over budget and anyway she should think about going home soon now that her assignment was over. If she wanted to stay in England, he suggested that she find herself some part-time work to supplement her extravagant lifestyle.

'You heartless scunt!'

She slammed the receiver in its cradle, then enacted a replay of herself by picking it up and slamming it down again. The children tittered. She wagged her finger at them and told them if she ever heard them use that word she'd wash their mouths out with soap and wash their gall with a good hot licking.

The phone box was opposite a small newspaper and confectionery outlet. She read the minds of her children when she said they could go in and each choose a packet of crisps. Three rings pressed her body from her knees up to her

137

waist, then pats and shouts of 'Yippee', then nothing as her boys tore from her and ran into the shop. While they hesitated over which flavour to choose, her eyes strayed from magazines she couldn't afford to the notices in the shop window. One card described a lost kitten as a treasured companion and friend. The campaign secretary shuddered. Another wanted to exchange a house in the town for a bigger house outside the capital. She tut-tutted. A third offered a new cot and pram and some toys at a price which seemed reasonable. There was an added handwritten note in brackets under the typed inventory and asking price with the underlined heading 'reason for sale'. The campaign secretary frowned but read on. The crude script said 'our baby died'. She gasped and had to cover her mouth. She held on to the counter until the sudden fog before her eyes cleared.

'You all right, love?' The shopkeeper peered into her face. She saw herself reflected in his thick spectacles, smiled as best she could and nodded vigorously as she pretended to read the notices, but her eyes saw a pram and cot of her own and swaddled in it the girl child, her third child, she had had to bury.

She dabbed the corners of her eyes. Then she went over to her children, who were picking up packets of crisps and putting them down again after looking at what the others had selected. She picked up three bags at random and stuffed them into their hands. The children complained bitterly as she paid at the counter. She avoided the shopkeeper's eyes by looking into her purse as if she were reading fine print and then by glancing at one of the more harmless notices in his window. She read, 'Earn in your own home as you watch over your kids. Sewing machine and training provided free.' She smiled at the shopkeeper and asked him if he could spare his pen for a moment for her to jot down a number. As he hunted around for one and came up with a piece of paper too, the three boys took their crisps back to the shelves and quickly replaced them with the flavours they preferred. They were back by her side by the time she'd copied the number and returned the pen to the shopkeeper with profuse thanks and smiles.

A man was using the phone. The children shuffled beside their mother and watched each other to see who would be the first to open his crisps. When the man came out of the phone box he held the door for her. She thanked him and allowed the boys to troop in before her. They held their crisps above their heads to protect them as they squashed together. 'Keep those bags quiet while I'm talking or I'll put them back on the shelf.' Crisp-packet crumpling ceased but the bearers seemed to be holding their breaths too. She dialled and looked down at her flock in various attitudes of stillness. 'Breathe, you little dodos.' A man with a deep, sonorous voice and a heavy accent she couldn't place asked her for her name and address, enquired how soon she'd be home and promised to have one of his men there in an hour.

On the brisk walk back to the house the youngest succumbed to the temptation of his crisps and tore open the packet after a struggle. The contents spilled out. He stopped in his tracks, stared at his crisps on the pavement and wailed. Right away his two elder brothers opened their packets and loaded his bag back up to its full complement. The campaign secretary patted them on their heads and swept up the youngest in her arms. As they picked up their pace, two pigeons swooped down on the free booty.

She explained the situation to the children as they approached the house. A man was coming with work for her. They would be able to ride once more on the Big Red Vroom Vroom and perhaps even on a train. But she needed their help to tidy the living room since she had to make space for a sewing machine that would require as much room as the television. The boys exchanged alarmed looks. The second youngest nudged the eldest to speak up. He asked what would happen to the television. She laughed. Nothing. She said they had one-track minds. She lamented the fact that they did not apply the same guile when it came to learning to read and write. Whatever guile meant, thought the eldest, it was good. Guile, thought the second youngest, was not the thing that would be washed with a licking, that was gall. Their mother always said, 'Wash your gall', or what he and his brothers referred to as 'Lix like peas'. The youngest said out loud as he bounced in his mother's arms, 'Guile, guile, crocodile.' The other two took up the chant and skipped along to keep time. A few steps from the front door she put down the youngest and got him to skip with her. She paused with the key in the latch to remind them of the curfew against any loud noise in the house. Then she felt under the bed and when her hand hit a brown box she smiled and went back into the corridor to close the front door and herd the children into the living room.

She was still stuffing clothes and shoes into boxes and pushing them under the bed when a red van pulled up outside. There were three rapid knocks on the door. She pictured a little, dumpy, hard-faced man behind that knock, who would stare along his nose at her and speak to her as if she had the IQ of a hamster. So many of that type occupied positions of distinction in the government. So many of them had treated her with the kind of cursory bad manners associated with a visiting dignitary. Or else they'd pursued her with a loquacious charm that would not take no for an answer. None of them had endeared her to the government. Her loyalty was to the President. His speeches had made her cry. He had instilled in her a belief that everyone could contribute to make the country the most prosperous in the region. But he had also said that too much had been achieved to hand over the reins to a bunch of amateurs. To lose the country now would be to lose everything they'd put into building it over the last five years. One more term in office would guarantee the loyalty of all voters in the country. To secure that second term, certain acts of courage would be required of the party faithful. If he had asked her at that moment to walk into the sea she would have found her way to the sea wall through her tears. All he'd asked was that she procure some votes from abroad. A small contribution to the country's future in her view, small but significant.

She tried to get a look at her visitor through the two strips of smoked glass in the door but decided to open it when she realised that he could probably see her outline standing there. She opened the door, took one look at the man and promptly shut it. 'Who are you?'

He was her age, mid-twenties, the height of her husband, six foot, but with long, curly, black hair swept to the left of his forehead and shadowing his left eye. He could be from India, or Saudi Arabia. He had a dimple in his chin and a little mole on his left cheek which was overshadowed by the long, straight bridge of his nose.

'The sewing man. You called us not so long ago. Here's my ID. I'll pass it through the letter box.'

By this time the boys had left their station on the bed to see who had caused their mother such consternation. She pointed to the bedroom and widened her eyes at them and they scrambled out of sight. The clean, pared nails of three fingers poked through the letter box clutching a laminated photograph of the face she'd just glimpsed. There was his name and that of his company. She felt a flush of shame at her reaction to the stranger. Taking a deep breath, she pulled the door wide and smiled.

'Welcome, Mr Ahmad. Sorry about that.'

'Oh, no no no, nonsense. You can never be too safe these days.'

He shook her proffered hand the way her husband's mother shook out mats over the verandah. He brought a large black bag with him. She led the way into the living room while she massaged her hand. He asked her if she planned to sew in the other room but she pointed to a space near the window and he nodded and said he'd fetch the machine from the van. She offered to help him, he thanked her and insisted that she would be most helpful if she held the doors open for him. Suit yourself, she thought, slip a disc, see if I care. This brand of chivalry was reminiscent of certain civil servants in the government who delegated responsibility to men junior to her on the basis that the pressure would strain her brain. Where would she be now if she had stayed with Dentist Richmond?

He brought in a large metal frame with a pedal, went out again and returned with the machine, which was compact but clearly heavier than the frame, going by the redness of his face and the prominence of a single vein on his forehead which ran from his right eyebrow up to his hairline. He slotted the machine into an open square at the top of the metal frame. Again he went out to the van and came back with a can of oil, which he poured into a compartment of the machine. When he knelt with the plug and searched for a power point she realised how idiotic she'd been. He asked her if she had an extension cord. She said no but she would move the television out of the way and put the machine there. He said he couldn't deprive her of her television viewing. She complained about the fact that there was only one outlet in the entire room. He said he had two things in his van he would let her borrow only if she promised not to tell his brother that he'd done so. She crossed her heart and he came back with a triple socket and an extension cord.

The curtain separating the living room from the bedroom twitched as the little fingers of the boys parted it further to get a clearer view of the man who was making their mother laugh. The eldest wondered if their father ever made her laugh like that. He hadn't witnessed it. He had seen her cry because of him, but not laugh. She'd cried when he left the house at Ariel and cried again when he did not return. If she laughed like this with this new man, did it mean that he would be their new father? No, there would have to be laughter but there would also have to be love. Laughter always came first because laughter was easy. Love was harder. Getting a new father would be impossible because of it, love. But he wanted one anyway. Not for him but for his younger brothers and, most important of all, for his mother. They played together but their mother had no one her age with whom she could play. She laughed with them often. Why was this laugh different? She covered her mouth and seemed to blush. When she laughed with him and his brothers she never covered her mouth or blushed.

'Boys, come and meet Mr Ahmad.'

They edged around the curtain vaudeville-style, an encore of some kind on their mind. But they were shy; this was the first time they'd met someone in the house apart from the owners. Mr Ahmad threw open his arms and lunged towards the children. They took two steps back in unison, tripped on the curtain and fell, bringing it down on top of them. Six little hands and feet tousled beneath yards of cloth. The campaign secretary snatched it off them as a magician would in the culminating gesture of an elaborate trick. The youngest was about to cry but when he saw his brothers giggling, he laughed. He glanced at his mother. She was laughing with her hand over her mouth. She'd turned a shade brighter than the crimson velvet curtain.

Mr Ahmad apologised to the children for scaring them and he blamed himself for the broken curtain rail. Taking one look at the rafter from which the curtain had been happily suspended until his arrival, he apologised again and said he'd fix the damage right away. She tried to tell him it didn't matter but he was insistent. He left the room and returned with his toolbox in one hand and a small step-ladder in the other. Putting them on the floor, he turned to the children. He held up two empty palms to them and swivelled his hands to show their backs hid nothing either. Next, he pulled a handkerchief from the top pocket of his jacket and spread it over his left hand. Then he opened and closed a fist several times in rapid succession over the covered hand. At last he pulled the handkerchief away with a flourish to reveal three tubes of Smarties. The children's mouths were open wide for so long a fly could have zipped in and out of each in turn. Mr Ahmad offered them one tube each, starting with the youngest, while the campaign secretary applauded.

'What do you say, boys?'

All three uttered a roughly synchronised, 'Thank you, Mr Ahmad.'

Mr Ahmad positioned his ladder, took a hammer and some nails and ascended three steps. He loaded the nails, head-first, between his lips, and drove them one by one into the rafter with a few loud knocks applied to each one in a brisk, unceremonial fashion, until there was none left in his mouth.

'I'll make some tea.'

'No tea for me, I'm Muslim, but some hot orange would be fine.'

'Hot this, hot that. It's the only way to keep warm in this country.' She skipped out of the room and returned from the kitchen with a tray of glasses of hot orange for everyone. She signalled to the children to sit. They were still watching each other to see who would be the first to succumb to the temptation of his Smarties. The youngest invariably lost the waiting contest. The campaign secretary asked the eldest for one of his Smarties. He forced an obliging smile and surrendered his box to her. She asked him to open it and take out two for her, just two. With a look at his brothers, he flipped off the top and turned the tube until two fell into his mother's open palm. She pelted them into her mouth as if

144

they were two aspirin. Next she turned to the second eldest and repeated her request. He too was delicate and slow with his Smarties as though he were emptying sulphuric acid from the tube. Then she asked the youngest and helped him pour two from his tube.

Mr Ahmad offered to hang the curtain for her. The campaign secretary was quick to turn him down. She told him to drink his orange juice while it was hot and she would hang the curtain. The second she climbed the ladder she saw her mistake. The eyelets in the rail seemed to shrink when she raised the hooks on the curtain to them. She felt she was stretching towards something that was retreating. Her discomfort and his silence made her sure he was looking at her body. She became agitated. He knew she lived in a partitioned room with three children. He'd probably surmised from her circumstances that a man wasn't around. She glanced down with a nervous smile already in place. He was sitting cross-legged on the floor with his back to her, talking to the children, who were each offering him their tube of Smarties.

She coughed. 'Now for the sewing.'

Springing to his feet, he ran his hand through his hair and told her he'd been in her house for an hour and hadn't said a stitch about the sewing. She countered with the fact that while he might not have said a stitch about the sewing, he'd made three, no, four garments of friendship in the kindness he'd shown her and her children. He said those garments were plain and needed to be embroidered with an outing of some sort at a more propitious time. She nodded graciously. Was she a poet? Oh no, she said. At school she'd filled notebooks and her father was prone to memorising acres of Victorian verse, which he imparted to her in impromptu recitals that lasted for hours when most girls her age were playing with dolls, but that was years ago and, anyway, she hadn't the first idea what constituted a poem these days.

And he? He said he knew by heart most of the great Iqbal because Urdu was the greatest language a poet could work in – or with, he wondered. Both, she said.

She got two chairs. He showed her how to thread the machine. Then he unthreaded it and watched her get it right the first time. He told her she was a fast learner. She said he was a good teacher. Next he took two pieces of cloth from the black bag.

'The lighter shade is the bottom. This diamond pattern should be on the outside. They're blouse collars.'

He sewed one with the same deft actions used to produce the Smarties. Then he unpicked his handiwork by simply cutting the thread in a couple of places and pulling it out. He leapt from the chair and indicated with a sweep of his arm that she should sit. He stood to her left and leaned forward. She lined up the two pieces of cloth and put her foot down on the pedal; the machine roared, the needle rose and fell and the cloth was snatched and scrunched up by it. She apologised profusely. Again he unpicked the cloth and told her to imagine she was about to cut her children's fingernails. The pedal at her feet powered the scissors and the needle was the actual blade. Miraculously, her hands steadied and her feet became light. She was slow but completed the collar in a neat line.

'You are a poet.'

He applauded and the children joined in.

'Ring me when you've finished this lot or if you have any problems. See you in two days, if I don't hear from you.'

The children accompanied him to the door with their mother and waved to the red van. He tooted the horn and thrust his hand out the window as he drove away. They shut the door when the van turned out of their avenue and onto the busy main road.

As she checked the brown box under the bed, a scuffle broke out between the three boys over which Smarties box

146

belonged to whom. The boxes were empty but in different states of disrepair. She pulled them apart and captured the boxes.

'Right. Since you can't share them, none of you will have them.'

The bottom lip of the three-year-old began to tremble and his two big black eyes moistened, then his shoulders shook, water erupted from his eyes and a sob jumped out of his mouth. The other two followed. The noise was deafening. She slapped them on their rumps, pushed them onto the bed and shut the curtain behind her. As she settled at the sewing machine, she began to talk to herself. 'See what trouble your sweet-talking father landed me in. Three children with hard ears. Your no-good father. God, I'm glad I left him. You all could go and join him but he wouldn't have you. He rather have his women. I drop everything for him and look where it left me. All the trials I go through for you children and this is all the thanks I get. Bad manners, rudeness and stupidness. Just like your father. What a useless man. He did not defend me in front of his mother. He could talk a suicide off the ledge but he could not say a word to save his marriage.' She fell into an exasperated silence and found herself listening to the hum of the machine and then for any sign of the boys. They had gone eerily quiet. She tiptoed to the curtain and, looking round it, met three shocked mouths and three widened pairs of eyes peering up at her. Their little faces each boasted some feature or other of the husband she no longer wanted: a high-bridged nose, big, hold-all eyes, dimples, even his prominent forehead. She fought off an urge to slap them and forced a smile.

Uncle Ahmad

'MR AHMAD IS now Uncle Ahmad,' the campaign secretary briefed her children.

'Uncle Ahmad,' they repeated together. The announcement did not throw them. In the days following Ahmad's first visit, his calls to the front room had become more frequent and later at night. The regular bursts from the motor of the Brother sewing machine would cease and Ahmad's bass voice would take its place, interspersed with the soprano of the campaign secretary's giggle. Bass and soprano would lull the children to sleep on the double bed behind the heavy curtains that divided the room.

Occasionally, their sleep was broken not by the alternating words and giggles of bass and soprano, but by simultaneous moans and groans. The children called out one night, thinking perhaps the two adults they adored were choking on the fine dust shed by the fabrics that had taken over the room. This dust made the children sneeze between and in the middle of their words and food so that they'd taken to wearing handkerchiefs over their mouths and noses when awake and resembled apprentice bank robbers. The noises came to an abrupt end. The campaign secretary put her head round the curtain, using a section of it to shield her body as if she had lowered an opulent veil to reveal a bare neck and shoulder and no more. She told them everything was splendid and they were to go back to sleep like good children.

They tried but found themselves listening to the dark.

Soon the cacophony started again: bass words and soprano giggles succeeded by simultaneous moans and groans. The children lay still, strapped to the bed by the sound that acted on their bodies like layers of sheets tucked around them by a firm hand. Their mouths gaped for air suddenly scarce above the bed. The lids retreated from their eyes, baring gross amounts of white. Their hearts pummelled against their chests, reverberated in their ears and shook their bodies. Worried that the campaign secretary and Uncle Ahmad would be interrupted by three loud, irregular drums, they willed their hearts to quieten or stop altogether. The youngest of the three accomplished it. His heart slowed to such a drastic extent that the pulse in his wrist and neck could not be discovered. He mastered his breathing too, regulating it to the occasional intake of air.

With Uncle Ahmad's late visits, the fortunes of the children took a sudden upturn. There were regular visits to the zoo in his red van. At the zoo they named the animals and birds after their absent elder brothers and the cousins and uncles and aunts they missed. Bounce was a rhinoceros, Beanstalk a giraffe, Wheels a cheetah on account of his speed. Aunt Footsy had to be the bearded orangutan that peeled bananas with its feet while it scratched its head and armpits. Red Head was a parakeet, Bash Man Goady a marauding male elephant, partly because of its pronounced genitals. They'd decide on Granny and Grandad on a future visit. What they wanted but couldn't find were two extra special animals. Nothing a zoo could contain. Something they might see in the shapes of clouds or if they linked the stars.

Saturday mornings the children were taken to the homes of Ahmad's Muslim friends in the East End. There they practised washing in the prescribed way. This was called ablutions, which the youngest always said as abbalusho-wons. Then they got into rows after an adult took a compass

149

reading and they all faced the direction indicated by the compass needle. This was called Kaaba. They did the same exercises as the adults to a rhythmic chant in a language they did not understand but would soon pick up. Sometimes they practised writing in patterns from right to left and learned a new alphabet. Say Arabic, not aerobic.

Over crisps, popcorn, Smarties and Pepsi, Uncle Ahmad explained circumcision. The children nodded to everything. It was hard to concentrate on the order in which they should eat all their treats, chew and listen. The youngest watched the eldest and nodded when he nodded. Seeing both of his brothers nodding made the middle child nod as well. It seemed the right thing to do. Their mother was pleased that the ramifications of the forthcoming circumcision had been explained with such facility by Ahmad. The children knew these two grown-ups were happy by the alternating bass and soprano of their voices. They were sure the voices would not suddenly become simultaneous moans since it was a public place and daytime.

Ahmad's long, curved nose tended to water in the open. On their frequent sightseeing trips a globule formed below its tip. When he felt it or it was pointed out to him, he'd produce a large cloth, the colour of the latest garment he was distributing to the houses for sewing, from his trouser pocket and snort into it. He was the only man the children knew who could perform the entire operation of opening the cloth with a rapid shake, manoeuvring his palm under it with little jerks exactly to the middle of it, blowing into his covered palm, wiping his nose clean and returning the cloth to his pocket after folding it, all with one hand.

Once in Trafalgar Square he said something in Arabic, stepped deliberately on two pigeons and sneaked the trembling bodies into a plastic bag. He told the astounded children and their mother that the meat was good for his elder brother's weak heart. Both the campaign secretary and her children had to sit down to recover. They sat on the church steps at St Martin-in-the-Fields and watched the people on the pavement. The children saw a parade of feet. Each foot belonged to Uncle Ahmad and every heel and sole slapped, clicked and cracked not slabs of stone but an unfortunate pigeon.

Ahmad said loudly, 'Children, pick one of the passers-by for an experiment.' He could make a person stumble by just looking at them, he declared. Then he stared and caused people to fall. Trilbys staggered. Berets slipped. He tripped up nattily dressed sports types who went red in the face. Their mother joined in the game. Ahmad even managed to upset a couple who walked in synchronised steps and they dragged each other down trying to stay upright. Everyone laughed so much they had to dry their eyes and clasp their stomachs. The trodden pigeons flew from their minds.

Circumcision Day arrived. The campaign secretary washed all the children herself. She supervised the pulling-back of foreskins and the bountiful use of soap and water. Circumcision, thought the children, must be a form of cleanliness. Uncle Ahmad surfaced in his van with sweets and tinned drinks. To be circumcised, thought the children, is to be clean for a picnic. But the evidence of the bleak day stated otherwise. It was too cold and windy for eating in the open. Uncle Ahmad aimed his red van towards a part of the city they'd not visited before. Terraced houses lined the streets just like the one they rented a room in except these were bigger and some were detached and more trees interrupted the city's unending concrete. They parked at a house that looked much like the others. The front window was filled with a branched candlestick holding several candles. At the door Ahmad introduced each of the children to a man with a hat that was ten times too small for his head. Mr Goldbourne smiled, half-bowed and grasped their hands and they felt at home. The children revised their definition of circumcision further still: an act of cleanliness, pertaining to picnics and the friendliness of strangers.

Mr Goldbourne approached the eldest of the children and asked if he would follow him. But the campaign secretary pushed the youngest forward, saying she'd prefer it if he worked on them in that order. Mr Goldbourne nodded, smiled and turned to the youngest, who took his hand gaily and followed him to a back room. Uncle Ahmad accompanied them. As Mr Goldbourne washed his hands, Ahmad hoisted the child onto a table covered with a plastic. 'Help Uncle Ahmad to undo your trousers for Mr Goldbourne.' An Anglepoise lamp and two long strips of fluorescent light made the room unusually bright. Mr Goldbourne washed with his back to them, showing his thin hair and the pin that held the little hat in place. Uncle Ahmad's nose was moist. It would need wiping soon.

A gloved Mr Goldbourne eased the boy into a reclining position while his trousers and underpants were pulled off by Ahmad. The boy glanced at the two men and at the door behind which his two brothers and mother must be seated. This has to be all right, he thought, otherwise his mother would intervene and Uncle Ahmad would not countenance it. He only shifted when he saw Mr Goldbourne lift a large needle in the air, flick his middle finger against it twice, then squirt a little fluid from it.

'Don't look,' Uncle Ahmad commanded gently, 'and don't worry.'

He tried to obey. He studied the white wallpaper patterned with blue flowers for anything out of the ordinary. Mr Goldbourne said he would feel a small pinch shortly. He noticed that the stems on the wallpaper had flowers at both ends. What type of vase could hold them, he wondered. What he felt was considerably more painful than a pinch. He screamed. Not a sound he intended to make, he was thinking more of an Ahh. He tried to move but Uncle

Ahmad had pinned his legs with one arm and his body and arms with the other. 'Please, Mummy!' he shouted and cried.

'That's it,' Mr Goldbourne said. 'No more pain, I promise.'

He focused with his eyes shut tight but could not feel anything in his crotch. An intermittent tug by Mr Goldbourne was the sole reminder that the area around his thighs existed at all. He opened his eyes and saw red around his numb thighs, copious amounts of red which Uncle Ahmad was busy mopping up. He saw a thin blade in Mr Goldbourne's hand and the tiny part of his body that had been severed from him. He thought he should pee. If Mr Goldbourne had left him anything, he should be able to pee with it. He strained but nothing came out. He decided to make his heart and breathing slow down to calm himself.

'Wake up!'

He ignored the urgent taps to his cheeks and the prising back of his lids.

'He hardly has a pulse!' Mr Goldbourne's voice had risen to a shriek. He told Ahmad to call an ambulance. 'He must be allergic to the local anaesthetic.'

Ahmad was puzzled. What could he tell Mr Goldbourne? The child's mother said he did not have any allergies. Ahmad called her and fought to control the panic in his voice. He told Mr Goldbourne that he could not remember the emergency number. Mr Goldbourne snatched the phone from him. The child heard his mother's approach. He took a deep breath and stretched but avoided looking at his crotch, which had begun to register a dull ache. Mr Goldbourne returned the phone to its receiver and mock-punched the child on his chin. 'You little rascal, you! You scared the living daylights out of me.'

Ahmad lifted the middle child onto the table and the campaign secretary led her other two away. She signalled to

Ahmad with a brush of her index finger over her nose and he performed a speeded-up version of his one-handed clean-up operation, snorting into the makeshift handkerchief with a total commitment of the body.

In the red van on their way home the contents of a plastic bag was distributed among them by their mother. Ordinarily this would have been more than sufficient grounds for unconfirmed joy, but they all ached between their legs and so took the treats with grudging and resentful faces. The crisps tasted sour; Smarties were plain; Pepsi like something produced by the gall bladder. They eyed the treats and then each other knowingly. Perhaps if they ate more it would make them numb and before they knew what was happening a friendly stranger would cut out their tongues.

'Why aren't you eating, boys?' Uncle Ahmad enquired in the rear view.

'Don't worry,' the campaign secretary explained. 'They play this game of not being the first to eat to see who can make his sweets last the longest.'

'Shut up!' the eldest snapped. His mother pretended not to hear. Ahmad smiled. None of the children wanted to be the first to cry. When the face of the youngest became contorted but not a sound issued from his lips, the other two did nothing to wipe the water flowing down their cheeks. The eldest shouted, 'Mummy, we are dying!' Ahmad braked and slowed the van to a crawl.

'Be brave for Mummy,' urged the campaign secretary.

'No!' protested the second child.

Their mother's face reddened. She leaned over and handed the eldest a small bottle containing a white powder, telling him that since he was acting like such a big man he should apply it to his crotch and that of his younger brothers.

'I can't look,' he said to the second eldest. 'Direct me.'

The younger brother dried his eyes and leaned close to the

crotch of the eldest. The youngest momentarily forgot his distress and leaned closer still. The eldest braced against the seat. He turned his face towards the back door of the van. One hand gripped the seat while the other held the bottle above his crotch and waited on directions. 'Left. Left. Stop. Right a bit, stop. Left.' The second eldest took the bottle from his elder brother's hand and poured the powder on the afflicted area. Then he passed the bottle to his eldest brother and sat back for his flaming crotch to be doused by the powder. The eldest brother, who was already smiling in delightful relief, administered the magic concoction to first one crotch, then the other. When Ahmad looked in the rear view they were scoffing their goodies and wincing only when they forgot their common ailment and inadvertently brought their thighs together. They understood that circumcision was sweetness, then betrayal and pain beyond belief.

The next few days were spent recuperating in bed and in front of the TV. They moved around bow-legged with feet wide apart. Whenever they walked towards each other they'd stop and challenge each other in a long Southern drawl, 'You wanna draw?' They held their urine to minimise the excruciating burn it caused whenever they peed. To take their minds off the complaints of their pressurised sphincter muscles they conjured up images of solid objects and restricted their vocabulary to words that bore no relation to water. The second day of their confinement was the most miserable. It rained all day and all the programmes on the television seemed to be about water. When there was not rain there were simulations of it: their mother's sewing machine sounded like a downpour on a slate roof, and even the flames from the heaters dotted around the room conspired to sound like drizzle. Ahmad visited with sweets and flowers and before the campaign secretary could warn him, he asked, within earshot of the children, for a vase with the dreaded substance. The children ran, bow-legged as if in a bag-race, to the toilet and directed their high-pressure hoses at a picture of Uncle Ahmad all three had conjured up in the bowl. They dried themselves with excessive tenderness and much sucking of air and contorted faces and left the toilet for someone else to flush.

On the third day of their recuperation Ahmad appeared with an expensive box of Swiss chocolates and asked the campaign secretary to marry him. 'You can be wife number two.'

She fought back a sneer and converted it into a noncommittal smile. She and the children had first learned of Uncle Ahmad's other family when clothing they'd outgrown was stuffed into plastic bags by him 'to send home'. Until then the children had assumed that they were the only ones who had left people they loved in a faraway place called home. They had heard of India through the films they were accustomed to seeing back in the republic, but never of this other place carved out of it. The children asked him what films his Pakistan made in order to gauge for themselves its importance. When he said none he could name, they couldn't fathom why he even wanted to remember the place. He enthused about the heavenly beauty of the north of the land. Mountains, rivers and a variety of flowers, fruits and trees and cloud you can reach up and pluck. He said northern Pakistan (and he patiently taught them how to pronounce the names Muzzaferabad and Kashmir) was God's way of giving men a taste of the paradise that awaited them in the afterlife.

'Slavery ended long ago,' would have been her last words on the matter but Ahmad persisted. The campaign secretary said she had never in her life been anything less than equal to a man. To end that by becoming his second wife was in her books 'plain foolishness'. She told Ahmad about her first and current husband, 'that long streak of misery'. How he would disappear into the bush for up to six months, prospecting for diamonds. How he'd return to impregnate her before taking off for another prolonged spell. She left him, she said, even though she still loved him, after her discovery of a gem he had kept from her for years. He became sick with a bout of yellow fever. For six months he could not return to the bush. She cared for him, their children and the youngest, who had just been born. 'One day I answered a knock on the door and was confronted by an Amerindian woman and four hungry children enquiring if her children's father, her husband, was alive or dead.'

He abandoned his bush family too and was now somewhere in what the campaign secretary called 'this godforsaken country'. When she first arrived she could barely suppress an impulse to arm herself with a bar of soap, a bucket of water and a wire brush to scrub England from top to bottom. Instead she was here on government business with hardly enough funds to get even this basic equipment for her mission of giving London a facelift. Ahmad asked what government business, but she said she couldn't go into it now. She was grateful to Ahmad. He kept her company. He was kind to the children and made them happy. He'd introduced the discipline-inducing faith she'd feared the boys would not find in a country where the children swore at their parents and still had teeth in their mouths.

'Let me think about it,' she ended up saying, which Ahmad assumed was as good as a yes. 'Anyway, I'm not divorced yet.'

'You're divorced in your heart, that's all that matters.'

She wanted to reply that she wasn't in love yet either, but thought better of it. The boys had stopped asking about their father after she'd brushed their queries aside with, 'If it was left to him, all of you would be in your graves.' She said she hadn't the foggiest notion where in England he might be living. 'He's hiding with a lot of people's money while his children are hungry.'

The children's wounds healed. They celebrated by having a water-spout fight. Apart from getting as many references to water as possible into their talk, they swallowed large quantities and when it was time for their communal bath they sprayed one another with pale urine. They were glad there was no foreskin to retract to wash away the deposits they called 'cheese'. To them the man with the scalpel was a type of barber whose work could never be undone. They were therefore happy that his back-room artistry was not a disaster. 'English girls, here we come!' the eldest shouted, waving his water spout at the bathroom window. He pointed it at his brothers, who shielded themselves. 'Look at the smiling mouth,' he insisted. Then they turned to examining each other's armpits, top lips and chins for the first sign of hairs. They made a lather with the soap and decorated their faces with white beards and moustaches and their chests and crotches with frothy, bubbly hair.

A telegram from the embassy forced the campaign secretary to drop her sewing and leave the children unsupervised. She examined it with disdain and sucked her teeth loud and long. 'Stay away from the heaters in case you burn down the people's house.' At the phone box she had to wait for a teenager who was giggling and spitting down the receiver. The campaign secretary tried to hurry her along by standing in her field of vision; but whenever she was positioned in front of her, the girl would turn her back. After another ten minutes of waiting she flung open the door of the call box. 'Move your bony backside before you and I walk down the road today!' This produced the desired effect. The girl dropped the receiver, edged out of the box and ran off. She dialled. 'I got your telegram.' An embassy official took her number. She replaced the phone and waited for the return call. A young man with close-cropped hair sneered at her but she did not notice him. She was hoping for good news: some money and a firm booking of her passage and that of her three young ones to reunite them with their two older brothers.

It barely rang before she snatched it up. She knew it was an overseas call because of a hum which reminded her of listening to the sea with a shell to her ear, miles inland from any sea. 'What are you trying to do? Shame us? Some of these names look and sound like obvious concoctions, back-to-front names, names that sound like the whole family is voting.' She recognised Brukup's shrill note. His was the last voice she expected or wanted to hear. She remembered him from her days as Dentist Richmond's assistant. Brukup had the best teeth she had ever seen; not a single filling and each tooth perfectly proportioned. It was said that if a woman looked at his mouth and was able to blot out the rest of his body, she could love him. All the dentist had to do was polish a little. He complained happily that Brukup reduced him to the status of a shoeshine. When she handed Brukup the cup for him to rinse she would see his teeth at close quarters and experience a powerful urge to unclasp her brassière and lower one of her breasts into his mouth. To break the spell and retain her self-control she had to glance at his shrunken legs. Dentist Richmond used a mould of Brukup's teeth to remodel the mouths of ministers who came in with rotten teeth, inflammations, abscesses, teeth that were so loose in their beds that a child could lift them out and gums so putrid they emitted a flammable gas.

The campaign secretary steadied herself by leaning against the phone box. 'The President himself commented on it when he was going over the UK and US lists. He's so furious with you, you'd better not set foot back in this place.'

The young man with the sneer knuckled the square of glass nearest to her face. Without even looking at him, she shot him a rude sign with her middle finger. 'Brukup, when was the last time you or the President, for that matter, were in England? All the people have two first names and they all sound as if they're related.'

Silence greeted her and then the sound of air sucked between the teeth. 'The President was so mad he ordered me personally to dispose of the papers with your stupid names.'

She became angry. 'What! All of them?'

'No. Just the incredible ones.'

The door of the phone box opened and the line went dead. She turned her head slowly to give her time to compose some suitable insult. She jerked round fully when her eyes met not only the young man she was anticipating, but also a middle-aged man and the teenager she'd ejected earlier. She replaced the receiver wondering what to do next. A number of hands grabbed her and dragged her out of the phone box. The man, who must have been the girl's father, punched her in the stomach. As she doubled over he held her upright for the girl, who punched her several times in the head. Then he pushed her to the ground. All three closed in with their legs swinging. The campaign secretary screamed, covered her head and drew up her knees. The newsagent came out of his shop and shouted the man's and the girl's names. The young man went into the phone box and the girl spat at the campaign secretary, then followed her father and the newsagent into the shop.

She straightened herself as she hurried home, pausing at the door to dry her eyes. The children ran into the passage to meet her. When they saw her the joy dropped from their faces, succeeded by worried looks. 'Who upset you, Mummy?' She shook her head and smiled. The two youngest children took one of her hands and led her into the front room, the eldest trooped behind. She postponed all thoughts about how to break the news to the children that they wouldn't be going home for a long time and that she did not have the fare to bring their two brothers over to join them.

'Spit on your coat, Mummy.' She whipped off her coat and stared at the slimy mixture with her mouth turned down. 'These English phone boxes so dirty you can't even lean against the walls.'

Cuffs and Collars

A HMAD APPEARED, NOT to collect bags of completed collars and cuffs sewn through the night by the campaign secretary, but with three red bicycles for the children. They hopped on the spot and hugged him, clapped, hopped and hugged him some more. The youngest could not contain himself. The campaign secretary had to force him to go for a pee and change his trousers. Ahmad took a fourth bike from his red van and came back with a child. The boy stood in front of him. Ahmad urged him forwards with gentle pushes to his shoulders.

'This is Shaheen. My eldest son.'

But the boys were admiring the bikes and hardly seemed to notice. The campaign secretary was stern. 'Boys, introduce yourselves and shake hands with Shaheen.'

He had thick, black hair which he periodically cleared from his eyes in a sweeping action that mimicked his father's. He was the same age as the eldest of the three boys but taller and fleshier. They circled their bikes while he explained the gears and adjusted the seats to suit their legs. Then all four rode up and down the street on the pavement while the campaign secretary told Ahmad he should not have gone to the expense and that she had no way of paying him back. Ahmad said he was never interested in her money. He loved her and her poetry.

'Did I hear right what I just heard? Did you say poetry?'

'Sure. And love.'

They smiled into each other's faces. Ahmad told Shaheen

to take the boys to the local park and ordered them all to walk their bikes across the main road.

'Yes, Uncle Ahmad,' the boys said in unison, drowning out Shaheen's 'Yes, sir'.

'Will they be all right?'

'Of course, my boy is sensible.'

'I've never seen those children of mine so happy.' The campaign secretary wiped a loose tear from her eye. They waved at the children.

'What a beautiful child!'

'He takes after his father.'

They laughed louder and longer than his joke merited, without knowing or caring why. Ahmad led her into the house arm in arm. He closed the door to the front room, embraced her and kissed her. She was about to offer him some hot orange juice but he kept hold of her and prised her teeth apart with his tongue. The campaign secretary shot him a quizzical look, something to do with the fact that it was broad daylight and she wasn't in the mood, and besides, the children might suddenly return for some reason, but Ahmad was insistent. He held her tighter, thrust his hips into hers and worked her legs open with his right knee. The campaign secretary decided to count to three and then pull away from him. She reached one and found herself pulling his shirt out of his trousers. At two, she was trying to consume his probing tongue. She tried to think what came after two but her efforts to concentrate drew a blank. Several options suggested themselves to her; all had to do with Ahmad and the barrier of his clothes and hers.

Shaheen explained to the boys the exhilaration of the three hills he'd discovered a few days earlier at a dump near the park. The eldest said they'd enjoy the park today and the hills another time. Shaheen added that the biggest hill was called Tom, the middle hill, Dick, and the smallest hill,

Harry. He said riding down them was the closest they'd come to flying on their bikes. The boys mouthed the names, Tom, Dick and Harry. They slowed for the youngest, who rode a small bike with stabilisers. Shaheen asked them if they were interested in seeing these great hills. The boys said, of course they were, but they were supposed to go to the park, not some dump. Shaheen wondered if that wasn't an excuse; if the real reason wasn't that they were scared of the hills, especially of the biggest and steepest hill, Tom.

The eldest of the three made an abrupt stop. His brothers narrowly avoided crashing into him. He asked Shaheen if he wanted to fight him then and there. Shaheen, who had stopped several feet away, yanked his bike around and began to cycle back. The eldest leaned his bike against the wall of someone's front garden. His brother pointed out that it was stupid to fight the son of the man who has just given a bike to each of them. The youngest gave three emphatic nods. The eldest told his disapproving brothers to keep out of it, adding that he did not care if Shaheen was the prophet himself, an insult was an insult. Shaheen braked with his front wheel inches from the feet of the eldest and said he preferred to challenge him to a ride down Tom, Dick and Harry. The eldest accepted. 'Lead the way.'

They rode on the pavement in a line, weaving around prams and pedestrians, and if there was a tree, then riding on the slender pavement between it and the road; a trick the eldest told the youngest not to try because of the width of his stabilisers. At the main road the youngest followed the eldest while the middle brother paired up in front with Shaheen; finding it abnormally devoid of traffic, they rode across it and even lingered at the roadside for a few yards, hopping onto the pavement when they saw an articulated lorry approaching.

They paused at the entrance to the dump. The hills were higher and steeper than they'd imagined. Grass covered them, excluding a slim track that traversed each from top to bottom and linked all three.

'Let's start with Harry. Even your little brother can do that one.'

'Leave my little brother out of it.'

'But I want to.'

'But I want to,' the eldest jeered back. Shaheen led the climb to the top by sprinting more than two thirds of the way up before the precipitous gradient coerced him to a standstill, and then pushing his bike. He was matched by the eldest; the younger boys dropped off their bikes earlier, each at a lower point on the hill.

Love. His word, not mine, the campaign secretary thought. She saw herself perched on the lampshade above her reclined body, as it was being ridden by Ahmad on the sofa that was her bed. His sweat-polished back and bottom undulated. She confused his arms and legs with hers. Rather than untangling them into the correct pairings, she muddled them further, until they metamorphosed into an eight-limbed insect. This insect had two backs, she thought. Either it was struggling for air or in two minds about turning over. No, she was sure that was inaccurate. She had to amend it; but to what? She pondered the image of herself fused to Ahmad and their concomitant movements. One pair of lungs seemed to be struggling for air, as if crushed; the other panted out of sheer excitement. According to the insect's movements, the top half wanted, it would appear, both to separate from, and join onto, its lower half. Either the lower half of the insect wasn't having it, or the join wasn't a clean one, so the top half had to keep struggling. From the increasing speed of its movements the top half was getting frustrated with its efforts or building towards a successful join. When it stopped on the downward plunge of its rapid manoeuvrings, she imagined from her bird's-eye view that the insect's top half had succeeded somehow in making a kind of union. For both top and bottom halves of the two-headed insect were quite still, its eight limbs resting where they had fallen, half on, half off the sofa; its many lungs, breathing hard and fast, could be heard and discerned, lessening in speed and volume. Only after Ahmed got up from the campaign secretary was she able to slide off the lampshade with relief and glee and re-enter her body. The lampshade needed dusting. She had wanted to sneeze the whole time she was up there.

Harry proved accommodating. All four bikes swept down its slope and some way towards the summit of Dick. The children's eyes watered. Shaheen and the eldest of the three brothers managed to lift their feet off the pedals and stick their legs in the air. Talking too loud and interrupting each other as they talked, they scooted up Dick. At the top the youngest changed his mind and crawled down to about halfway, then mounted his bike and sped towards Harry. They waved to him from the top and turned for the descent. Shaheen cycled the first few yards to build up his speed and kicked his legs in the air but put them back on the pedals when the steering wobbled. His bike came to rest a little way up the side of Tom and he sat down beside it. The eldest brother pedalled too when he took off and learning, from Shaheen's example, he kept his feet on the pedals and worked them on the slow ascent of Tom. The second brother did not pedal and when he stopped he said he'd had enough excitement from Dick to bother with Tom. Shaheen and the eldest brother left him and climbed to the peak of Tom.

At its zenith both boys were meditative. They could see the youngest some way off crawling up Harry, and assumed from the middle brother's invisibility that he was some-where between Dick and Harry. Shaheen pushed off casually as if he were about to perform a chore he found tasteless but unavoidable. The steering wobbled but he straightened it and shot towards the level ground. He raised a fist in the air a few feet from the bottom and the front wheel veered to the left, then to the right and a third time to the left, but this time too sharply. The rear wheel rose into the air and Shaheen flew over the handlebars, hands thrust uselessly in front of him to break his fall. He bundled into the ground, rolled and lay still for a second, sat up quickly, grabbed his right arm and cried out.

The eldest ran down the hill to Shaheen's side. Shaheen asked him if the arm was broken. The eldest was astounded by this remark. 'Broken?' he repeated. 'Broken?' He would have added some insult had it not been for Shaheen's obvious distress. As a compromise he said, 'You fell off your bike, not a tower block.' This was a new word in his vocabulary, acquired when he accompanied his mother to view a flat the council had allocated to her, on the twelfth floor of an estate made up entirely of several towers. She wanted to take the flat for all the rooms it offered, but when she looked down from the window at the people below, she said they resembled ants and made her feel dirty, since she couldn't grab a broom and sweep them out of her sight.

The two younger brothers rode up and fussed over Shaheen, who did his best not to shed any more tears. The eldest brother retrieved his own bike from the top of Tom. He had the chance to ride it down but chose to walk, complaining as he approached that his concentration had been ruined by Shaheen's fall. By this time the younger two were brushing the sand and dirt from Shaheen's clothes. He thanked them through gritted teeth. His arm had swelled to twice the size of the other one and scared them all into hurrying back. The eldest rode his bike and pushed Shaheen's alongside. Shaheen sat in the saddle of the second brother's bike, balancing and nursing his arm, while the second brother stood and pedalled. The youngest stuck close to him.

Traffic on the main road was intermittent. The middle brother led. When he rode off the pavement, Shaheen cried out. He apologised, glanced up and down the road, saw that it was clear and headed for the other side. The eldest brother instinctively followed but had great difficulty controlling Shaheen's bike while steering and pedalling his own, after the jolt when he rode off the pavement and into the road. Nevertheless he closed the gap opened by his younger brother's rapid, albeit rough, progress and was almost at the other side of the road when he noticed a large lorry some way off and glanced round to make sure the youngest was close behind him.

'You didn't enjoy that, did you?'
    'What makes you say that?'
    'You seemed detached.'
    'Well, you're wrong. I enjoyed it very much.'
    'By the way, those collars and cuffs are sewn wrong.'
    'What! All of them?'
    'Looks like it. Look at the example again.'
    'I shall just have to unpick them and start again.'
    'You should marry me.'
    'And be wife number two? No thanks.'
    'Well, this arrangement can't go on.'
    'Look, I did everything you asked me to do. I became a Muslim. I dragged my boys into it. Then you tell me you're married and you're surprised I won't agree to marry you.'

Ahmad fell into a wounded silence and dressed. The campaign secretary felt irritable with him, a mood worsened by the prospect of unpicking one hundred and fifty collars and cuffs. She stepped into a yellow cotton dress and strained to reach the zip behind her back, having pulled it three quarters of the way up. Ahmad did not make his usual offer to help her with it, even though she reached over her shoulder with one hand, then the other, in full view of him, grasping at the air behind her back. She flushed with embarrassment at her failure to draw him into a renewed intimacy and became angry.

'Go and fetch the children from the park, please.'

'Only if you come with me.'

They looked at each other fiercely. Lacking further grounds on which to mount an angry exchange, with each second of silence that passed they found their tight expressions crumbling into unexpected smiles and, liking the alteration, laughed unabashedly and embraced.

'Marry me?'

'As soon as you get divorced.'

An urgent knock on the door punctured their taut repose. Ahmad opened the door and stumbled a couple of steps backwards when he saw Shaheen's outsize and purple arm. He recovered almost immediately, scooped up his son into his arms and ran to the van.

'I am taking him to Emergency.'

'I'll come with you.'

'No. You look after your boys. I'll be back.'

The campaign secretary demanded an explanation from the eldest. At his mention of the dump, she asked what dump when they should have been in the park. She called them a bunch of ruffians and assured them they were going to bed without supper. They put their bikes in the garden shed and she followed them from there to the bathroom, then to bed, railing against them throughout.

'You all so wild, like you grow up in the bush. No training. No common sense. Brand-new bikes and you gone to a dump to play. I wish to God you three had broken your arms. Your big brothers would be ashamed of all of you. Poor Shaheen! The damn boy will be in plaster for six weeks. What a blasted good-for-nothing bunch of children God give me! Why couldn't I have girls? Some sweetness in my life. Your uncle Ahmad should never have brought you those bikes, circumcision or no circumcision. You lot don't understand kindness. You spit in kindness' face. Your ears are hard. Your mouths need washing out with disinfectant. One squeak out of any of you and I'll wash all your galls tonight.'

Dusk cast everything in shadows. She moved to the window at the front portion of the room and watched an orange sky deepening to russet. Here, the sky looked dense and close compared with the sky in her republic. There, the sky was so far away, its clarity was sharp without being inviting; a sky that didn't give a damn whether you noticed its parade of colours or not, it was so sure of itself. Here, the sky hated to be ignored and did everything it could to earn its place at the centre of everything people discussed. She fancied that if this sky didn't like you it would drive you into the sea and over the edge of the horizon by simply lowering itself and threatening to crush you. There, if the sky hated you it simply retreated further, thinning the air more than the lungs could bear, leaving you breathless and lonelier than you ever dreamed possible.

Ahmad was good to her and the children but his proposal was impossible. She had no intention of being second anything. Then there was the inviolable question of her lack of love for him. There had to be love. Love or nothing. That was that. There were other men out there, without wives they wanted to supplement, who would be willing to take her on. They would find their way to her. All she had to take was a long view. She was young. Her children had aged her but they hadn't ruined her.

She felt Ahmad's semen running out of her cold and decided to perform her ablutions. Then, clothed from head to foot, she took her little compass from the mantelpiece and, using the orange streetlight soaking through the net curtains, found the direction of Mecca. She spread her red velvet mat with its likeness of the holy rock of Kaaba woven into it and prayed. She had memorised the Arabic in a Saturday class for children. She enjoyed mouthing its syllables, which she saw as smooth, round and colourful like the marbles her rotten children collected. She was reminded of the Victorian poetry she had heard her father recite as a child and whose meaning she comprehended only dimly, seeing in her mind's eye, and hearing too, during those inexhaustible narratives, riderless horses galloping over rolling countryside. Except that this poetry was God's, she reasoned to herself, and not man-made, and as if to confirm its holy origins to her, it came in a tongue she did not know but deemed beautiful and uplifting. Saying the prayer on her breath freed a section of her mind to which she would otherwise have been denied access.

After prayers she ran her palms along the smooth velvet of the mat. She smiled at its red changed by the orange light falling through her net curtains. At first the streetlight had been weak against light from the sun that had long buried itself in the sky. Then, as the sky had darkened and lowered its dark curtain, the streetlight had grown distinct. She folded the mat as if making an envelope and switched her attention to the sofa that doubled as her bed, still choosing to work by streetlight and hoping to see Ahmad's headlights soon. A bottom sheet was tucked around the cushions, followed by a top sheet, two blankets and a quilt. It was late spring but to her and her children's bones it felt like winter, necessitating all manner of hot drinks.

A peep at the boys showed them all limbs over each other and still except for a barely discernible rise and fall of their chests. She wriggled into the cool bed without disturbing her handiwork too much, accomplished by moving the pillow and snaking her way in feet-first. The weight of the blankets and quilt felt pure – a welcome contraint that did not impede

171

her diaphragm and ribcage. She did what she had always done last thing at night: tune in her portable radio to the World Service and spare a thought for her two eldest children and those three brutes behind the drapes, muttering in their sleep. She pictured all five of them together and smiled. Try and stay awake for the news, she commanded herself, but settled for the comforting notion that Ahmad's imminent return would wake her. Then she would be fresh for the lonely all-night combat with those collars and cuffs.

She glanced across the room at the luminous clock on the mantel above the redundant fireplace. At first she had to bury it under cushions to muffle its panicky, loud ticking, like an insect trapped in a box, until one day she didn't hear it any more. The hands and numbers seemed to float on the clock's face as if resting on a delicate current.

The next moment she was woken by the children crawling all over her. She sat up quickly and clawed at her face to clear it of the spider's web woven there by sleep overnight. The youngest toppled off her midriff onto the floor and glanced up at her with a startled face. Before he could convert his surprise to a loud wail, she scrambled him up, squeezed him in a tight embrace and shook him and her with rapid movements from left to right. She paused and looked at him and he smiled. To get him to laugh she buried her face in his neck and blew. According to the squirms and exclamations of the other two boys, the noise her action produced was obscene. The youngest shrieked.

'Good morning, my petals.'

'Good morning, Mummy.'

'Today we are going to the seaside.'

Shouts and hugs and leaps into the air lasted a full minute. She stood with her hands on her hips and watched them. Then the dreaded questions began. Was Shaheen all right? When would Uncle Ahmad arrive to drive them to the sea?

172

When, not if; that man has weaselled his way into my children's hearts, she thought. 'Just us this time.'

A curtain of gloom dropped across their faces, extinguishing the lights that had blazed there a moment ago. She sighed, a little defeated by the display of disappointment. This is what mothers have to put up with, she thought, ungrateful children and disappearing men.

'Listen, children. Uncle Ahmad and Mummy are not special friends any more.'

'But he's still our friend,' the eldest said, pouting.

'I know, darling. He will always be your friend. It just means we'll see less of him and do more things without him.'

Now they were crying and she was crying too – for them, for him. What must we sound like, she wondered, alley cats in a brawl?

'We mustn't keep the sea waiting. You can bury me in the sand and build sand castles.'

'Can we have ice cream?'

'Of course.'

'And candyfloss?'

'Yes.'

'And sugar apples?'

'Ice cream, candyfloss, sugar apples, sand castles, here we come!'

Once again they were dancing around her. She skipped around with them. They all froze at five loud taps on the ceiling from the landlord upstairs. Covering their mouths, they looked at each other and giggled. She put her index finger on her lips and the boys began to wade around the room in slow motion as if up to their chests in the sea. They wrestled into their clothes and watched their mother as she turned her back to put on her bra and step into panties. When she turned and knelt to tie the laces on the shoes of the youngest, the other two hugged and kissed her and it was as

173

if Ahmad had never existed, even though they were nowhere near the sea yet.

On the train to Brighton the children began their landscape game in earnest after she made them agree to settle all disputes with her, the great conciliator, latterly a campaign secretary, formerly prospective wife number two to Ahmad, now free and husbandless with three – no, five – fatherless boys, not on the lookout because men can be found at two to the dozen, yet walking towards men with eyes open wide and knees clamped together. When the eldest boy described something that was orange and landed in the sky even she couldn't guess. This called for a close inspection of the sky. She leaned towards the window and looked up. The sky was immense today and yet to her it seemed delicate and untouchable as a just-laid sparrow's egg. Nothing lands in the sky, she thought. The youngest two stared at her for assistance. She shrugged her shoulders and glanced quizzically at the eldest. He laughed, revelling in the knowledge that he'd not only caught out his two brothers but had stumped his mother too.

'What's orange and lands in the sky?' he asked aloud, this time as though to everyone in the carriage. He folded his arms and peered into the faces of his brothers and mother. If the other two were here, they would have solved it by now. Of that she was certain. What are those two up to now? Still calling each other those awful names and fighting? Bash Man Goady, Red Head. A general pain, located around her sternum, radiated outwards as high as her throat, where it deposited a lump, and to the pit of her stomach in rapid stabs with a blunt knife. She clutched her heart but pretended to adjust the left cup of her bra. The middle of her body felt hollow, as if she hadn't eaten for days. Every time she thought of her two boys she felt this pain. They were in her head with such regularity it was more like an occupation, so that the instances when she felt nothing were rare.

'The sunset is orange.' She whispered this to her youngest, who announced it to the carriage with a raised chin and a straight back.

'Wrong,' the eldest shouted. 'Give up?'

'Certainly not.'

'Certainly not.' The youngest echoed the middle brother.

Both stared at their mother for the solution. She scrutinised the sky. Perhaps a passing jet's vapour trail had written out the answer in letters that would soon disappear. She thought of her two boys. By leaving them behind she wondered if she hadn't written their names in lemon juice and watched the names dry to invisibility, but when she tried to restore what she'd written by passing it over a flame, instead of the heat clarifying the memory, gradually, magically, before the eyes, instead of preserving her boys in a safe and secret place for their resurrection, intact, at any time, they were lost to her, and there was nothing. Nothing. The flames simply consumed the paper. She brought herself back with a jolt, the kind of involuntary action credited by her to the fact that someone had just, at that moment, walked over her grave. There was orange in the sky but how it could have landed there was inscrutable to her.

'How about a clue, brain-box?'

He folded his arms tighter and fought to suppress a laugh but failed. A compressed smile played around his lips: tiny explosions deep beneath the skin that were visible as short-lived facial spasms. She wondered why this couldn't last. When, not if, she was reunited with the other two, she determined, they'd replay the whole scene as if for the first time. Back at the house she would still have to face the chore of unpicking those wrongly sewn cuffs and collars. The thought made her shudder.

'You all give up?'

'Yes.'

'You as well, Mummy?'

'Yes.'
'Fireworks. Fireworks land in the sky.'

That night, the boys were so tired she had to help them undress. The sand in their socks and between their toes would end up in the bed. Seeing herself lying on sheets riddled with sand put her teeth on edge. But they wouldn't mind. They were too tired to eat, much less wash. In no time she could hear their snores. Too exhausted even to look at the sewing job she had to put right, she made her bed on the couch in a hurry and lay on it, switched on the radio and looked at the light fixture over her, imagining a pendulum suspended by a cord from the ceiling. She and her makeshift bed, her children and that blasted sewing machine were all inside this giant clock, and responsible for its work. The pendulum would swing until sleep crept up on tiptoe, unobserved, and claimed her.

Fatigued as she was, sleep would not come, though she had made herself into its most welcoming receptacle, tucked in cosily. What crept up was the light. Grey at first but returning definition to things she knew in the dark and now could see. Grey, then white and with the white, intermittent vehicles, a dog and a passer-by whose footfall on the pavement was a metronome. Soon she would force herself to get up and attack those cuffs and collars, breaking her meticulous stitch in two places and pulling the entire thread clear of the cloth like a bird pulling a worm from a lawn.

IV

Dear Future

Dear Future

Dear Future,

You don't know me. We won't meet. Let me introduce myself. I wasn't christened or baptised. Someone, a mother or even a father, named me something or other, I forget what. Or else it didn't suit my new surroundings so it was quickly dropped.

My new family took a good look at me the day I arrived. In fact, they watched me for days. Watched how I crossed a room, a yard, a field. Studied which foot led when I jumped or swung my legs on a high chair and which hand was outermost when I folded my arms or clasped them behind my back.

They looked at me from head to toe like this as if they were considering an expensive purchase at the hardware store. Then one of them, the tall one I grew closest to, who nearly killed me, shouted Red Man and they laughed in recognition, then Red Head and their laughter grew and it stuck.

That's the name I wrote on my school slate on my first day at school and the only name I answer to now. Those who used my previous name and got no response from me came around to using Red Head soon enough; even those in authority relented. It feels like I've been no one but Red Head.

Dear Future,

Time ran out on me. I am free to address you as a lost chance rather than an eager prospect. You see, I am the second son of five boys so it's important that you get to know my elder brother, who is with me here in this ever-present past, and my three younger brothers, who are scattered somewhere in the wide pasture that holds you, the future.

My elder brother has not always been good to me. Now we are perfect friends and our love is broadcast regularly to each other. This doesn't stop us arguing for the sake of it. We argue over who started the argument. We argue about past disagreements. We even argue about the odds on who will start the next row in our present predicament. But there is love. He stands a good foot over me and he is strong, able to open jars I can't, breaking sticks I can barely bend and throwing a stone further than my best throw. This does not prevent me from wrestling with him. When he knocks me to the ground I bring him down with me by wrestling his legs from under him. When he sits on my chest and pins my arms to my sides, he looks at me for a while as if considering what to do next, then jumps off me, bored, and takes quick steps away.

We are two lion cubs left to fend for ourselves in a long wait for the return of our mother or even our father.

Dear Future,

Since you are what I can never become, hear me out. Find my mother and three brothers, give them some sign that my brother and I are fine. As fine as our new situation (which takes some getting used to) allows.

I wouldn't dream of asking you to do something you do not wish for me in this peculiar present of mine. Just give them a sign that there is no suffering where we are and that our love for them is as strong as when we were in a position to say it (though we never did).

I miss them because I perished missing them. My brother is the same. But he speaks as little about these things as he did when we thrived.

I saw a tree dripping with gum so I put some on a stick and displayed the stick in a prominent place hoping a bird of paradise will alight on it. My plan is to put the bird in a cage and listen to its song.

Dear Future,

Bash Man Goady has more mud balls than me. Somehow, when he passed me my slingshot and divided the mud shots between us, I was too grateful and too busy marvelling at the fact that he had been able to smuggle both of our slingshots and ammunition in the middle of all that commotion. I noticed too late that he had swindled me out of my fair share. What should I do? There's no fighting here; no serious disputes permitted. Just brotherly and sisterly love. So if you've been cheated like I've been, there's no recourse to a good old scrap in the sand and no higher authority at hand to bother with these trifles.

This means I'm forced to work out a plan that will deceive him into spending extra pellets on worthless targets and even up our numbers. My scheme must convince him that I am using as many mud shots as he. If this thing backfires on me he'll never trust me again, and here trust is everything.

Dear Future,

Have you located my brothers? My mother? Or my father? What sign did you convey to them of our in-limbo existence? Let me know that you are working on my behalf.

Am I asking too much? I would look for a change in the weather and take that as a sign but there is no weather as such here, just a placid sun.

I would dig in the ground until I came across some emblem in the ground or a sudden change in the composition of the soil, but nothing is ever buried here and the soil is dark and crumbly without end.

I would study myself for a change but without time nothing changes, including me.

No luck with my gum stick. The birds can smell a trap. I've moved it around, placing it in a favourite spot with the birds, but they've simply moved on.

Dear Future,

I've heard nothing from you, not a pip's squeak, so I've taken the initiative and written again. Am I a nuisance? My three brothers look nothing like me. I should have told you at the outset. There's nothing wrong with their looks but they're as different-looking as strangers because they, we, originate from two distinct races with contributions from two more thrown in for good measure.

What unites them and makes them my brothers is their attachment, and mine, to our mother. You'll know them when you see them precisely because of these acute differences.

On another matter, I pretended to fire a mud shot at the same time as my brother. He looked at me curiously when he saw that I'd gone through the motions of loading and firing at the same target and at the same time. He insisted that from now on I should fire before or after him since I ruined his aim.

Dear Future,

I was told I'd feel differently about relations on the other side once I grasped the workings of things on this side. Well, I know what's what here and I still can't bear to be separated from my mother and brothers. (And everyone at the big house, as a matter of fact, down to the animals and insects and air.)

I know they will do all the things I am unable to dream about even, because that's your nature, right? You give to one side what the other side has relinquished? But I still feel robbed.

How are they? I should believe they are well but the way I left that place has left me with the same fear for them. Tell me I am wrong to think and feel these things. I still can't talk to my brother, not even here. He's still inclined to assume the easiest outcome since that requires the least amount of his energy. I love him all the more. He is all I have here. Sometimes he seems to know me better than I know myself, then I remember that he has been with me longer than anyone, alive or dead.

Dear Future,

My brother insisted that we count up our mud shots, just to be sure he still had six more than me! I wanted to be mad but all thoughts here, the second they occur, are cancelled by an overwhelming feeling of love. So I told him I loved him and he knew I was annoyed. Nevertheless, he smiled and hugged me and over his shoulder I saw his big pile of mud balls outshining mine.

On the other side I might have tried to overcome this urge of mine to win every time. Here, I throw myself into it. Here, I feel everything I do or say is fixed for all time. The only thing that seems to increase is my knowledge of my faults. How can that be in a place where time stands quite still?

Dear Future,

Our mud balls have been classed as weapons. (Weapons of all kinds are forbidden.) We've been told to convert them into objects of love. It happened when we fired at what we took to be a statue of a bird of paradise at about the same time (Bash Man Goady fired a fraction before me as agreed) and both of our mud balls connected with the target and it fluttered to the ground.

Needless to say we were horrified and cried and immediately declared to ourselves that we'd done something terrible and came up with this solution to convert them. That is the way things work here. There is no judge and jury. Everyone comes up with the solution to anything unseemly that is suggested by a thought or action. We set our own standards in a place where the highest standard of all always prevails.

So we came up with this conversion thing. Now the idea of soaking these last mud balls until they become soft and misshapen, then mashing them into the soil, depressed us throughout the procedure, but we had no choice. In response to our unfortunate case of mistaken identity our consciences had invented the worst remedy possible in our eyes, yet one we could not help initiating and putting into effect. This is the nature of the place we're in.

Dear Future,

We'd done the opposite to get those mud balls round and hard. Hadn't we selected the clay by digging deep beyond the ubiquitous red sand? And hadn't we moulded each piece between our palms, which ended up clay-coloured, then arranged them on the corrugated zinc roof, like a battalion in formation for inspection, under the midday sun? And watched them harden from the comfort of a shade. And speculated about their fruitful application. For all that industry to come to this by means suggested by ourselves!

But that was on the other side where all things are possible. I'm not sure I like this place. I'm certain this place hates me. You know how a place can tell you that you don't belong in it? Every day I have to start from scratch in it. There is nothing around me to show that I belong. It's like a pit stop but without that race against the clock. I haven't clapped my eyes on one thing of which I can say, Ah, this is so-and-so. That's because nothing is anything here.

Dear Future,

Still zippo from you about my mother and brothers. I know you are working hard on my behalf. I hope you'll understand my persistence and tolerate me some more. You are my only option.

One good thing about these mud balls we had to destroy, sorry, I do mean convert: it drew Bash Man Goady and me closer than ever, united in our common opposition. To have had to unstring the sturdy V-shape of our catapults and mash that clay back into the ground destroyed or converted the last link maintained by us with the other side.

We cried like kittens and without shame for our mother. We meowed, 'Mummy! Mummy! Mummy!' In an alley someone would have thrown up a window and emptied a basin on us.

Dear Future,

Since you are beyond me I suppose I shouldn't keep anything from you. Answer this. If Sten is not here and she was the last person I was with on the other side, then where is she? I mean, precisely the same circumstances took us from Ariel and at exactly the same moment. Has she gone to some other place? Some opposite of here? Surely not? Surely Sten deserves to be here, with me, if anyone does? Where's the love in a decision like that? If my younger brothers had been with me at the time, where would they be now?

Dear Future,

I don't dream here. I conjure events that run alongside whatever is unfolding before my eyes or preoccupying my body. My mother and father were together in one of these conjurings. They were spreading a tablecloth that had been ironed moments before by Mummy, so that it was still warm, on a table which they proceeded to set for five children and two adults.

It occurred to me, seeing them before me like this, positioning forks, knives and spoons, plates, cups, saucers and even glasses, that I'd never, in my whole little life, witnessed this scene in actuality.

I told my brother and he was surprised, not by what I revealed, but that I bothered to do so at all. Apparently, he hasn't conjured a single event or person from the other side since our arrival here.

He wasn't pleased. I suspect he wanted to be the first to have conjured a parallel life alongside the one we have here. Tough big brother. I love you.

Dear Future,

My three younger brothers will give off an air of reliance on older siblings. You'll find them doing one predictable thing for a long time before switching to something else equally predictable. What you'll see is them playing it safe.

This is because everything Bash Man Goady and I represent has to do with adventure – at least in their eyes; things we consider quite ordinary, like hitting a bird on a fence with a slingshot from twenty-five yards.

Oh, a slingshot, a slingshot
I wish I had my slingshot
The things I would do with a slingshot
The places I would go with a slingshot
What a lot I could do with a slingshot
Oh, a slingshot, a slingshot.

I have time on my hands.

Dear Future,

My brothers are not dull. They are well-behaved. Put yourself in their shoes (as they will surely place their feet in yours) and imagine the strangeness of England – not only the big city, but fog. I warned them about fog to prepare them for the shock of it. I told them everything I'd heard about it. That it was like a cold steam that lingered until the sun drove it away. I told them fog was the city coming to life in the night and taking most of the next day to settle down again.

'Make sure you keep on breathing in fog. Breathe through your nose so you can filter it. Never breathe through your mouth.' Have they heeded my warning? I pointed to the pastures where the mule was grazing and I said, 'Swap all that out there, all those trees and grass and put concrete in its place and you have a city.' I told them they were very lucky to be seeing such a place.

Bash Man Goady warned them not to talk to strangers no matter how friendly they appeared. He showed them how to grab an adult between the legs in such a way that he would release his hold on them. They were to eat everything they were fed if they wanted to be big and strong like him and smart like me. He said that. Then we hugged them, gave them our choicest marbles, hugged Mother too. She said much the same things to us as Bash Man Goady had said to the boys and they departed in a car.

All three were lined up in the back seat waving in the back window until the car left town. The youngest was steadied between the other two. They must have instructed him to wave and keep waving. Wave at Bash Man Goady and Red Head. He was watching their hands to make sure he was doing it right rather than watching us.

I wanted to walk along a London pavement in thick fog seeing a couple of yards ahead, no more, with the fog on my shoulders and at my heels and my brothers strung out on either side of me. I was ready to give up all that grass and those trees, and Sten, for concrete, just to be with them. Everything about my life at that time informed me that if I could be with my immediate family, London would be mine, in all weathers. But everything I did not know about, because I was too small, conspired to keep me from it.

Dear Future,

In my daydream of you I am flying above cloud. I am about to be reunited with my mother and brothers. Miraculously, Sten is on my left, Bash Man Goady on my right. Both are looking out of windows at those clouds and once in a while they'll look at me and smile. We say nothing. Don't ask why. It's as if we've said all there is to say, and now, at this point, we can relax and view the unfolding of our destiny.

How we are being conveyed, I don't know. There is no sense of forward propulsion, just cloud vistas. Tell me, was it all simply a daydream? Was this your way of telling me I have not arrived where I am supposed to be but have merely paused, at a watering hole, as it were, to recuperate? Where are we going that requires flight at such a heady altitude?

Where else but to London to be reunited with Mother and Shick-shank, Big Forehead and Bellows? Although they're not aware of it, they've been christened by us in their absence, based on how we remember them. That was one of the long-standing arguments my brother and I had there, where there should be an end to argument, coming back at the same notion until it had been tested to death, knowing even as we argued that there was no other way to settle something as critical as a name, regardless of the fact that we were in a place where rowing was not the done thing.

We called it play. Shick-shank is shifty and shy with two turned-in feet and big, devouring eyes. He has black, curly hair and well-defined, black eyebrows that are straight for the most part, then suddenly, unaccountably, slope downwards.

Big Forehead seems self-explanatory but add to that protuberance a shine and a smile with dimples that can dissolve the most vicious intentions aimed at it.

Bellows is heard before he is seen, though he is the youngest. His voice was broken from the first day he spoke. His first word was shouted, 'Mummy!' His voice was so loud I was tempted to check behind him for a concealed adult speaker.

Dear Future,

Bash Man Goady wondered what kind of a place would separate children the way this place has divided us from everyone else in that back room at Ariel. He set me thinking about the other place where they must be right now wondering about us. I wonder which of us is in heaven, which in hell? Separation is hell and everlasting separation is death.

We have since regretted destroying or converting our mud balls and our slingshots. Our oath to ourselves is to build both again. Trouble is, the wood here is soft and the soil lacks body. Add to that a sun that sits uselessly in the sky and is more decorative than anything else.

We will have to procure fire to bake that clay (if we can find any) and locate a tree in this Eden with wood hard enough to absorb pressure when thinned.

Where is that soil or that wood in this place?

Dear Future,

Don't let me down. If Sten and the others are not here, maybe Bash Man Goady and me are the only two who crossed over. In that case, go directly to Ariel and let anyone you meet know that we are waiting to be rescued from here or to receive permission to leave or desire to be returned.

We are fine, tell them, but stuck. Happiness is fine but it takes you nowhere, it's like boredom. The future, any future, should at least improve on them.

Why, then, do you do nothing for me?

Dear Future,

As we suspected, every attempt to convert this soil into mud shots ends in failure. It is as if the soil has a will of its own. This must be a good place for someone.

We have examined countless trees for a limb. There is no shortage of perfect V's here. Catapults grow on trees. But they are all soft, offering little or no resistance. They cannot launch air, never mind a mud ball.

We found our old catapults where we had dropped them. At first we were delighted, until we picked them up, brushed off the growth of buds and roots (everything grows here) and could see they had become soft as a result of contact with the soil.

I'm afraid to stand too long in one place in case I begin to put down roots! Sometimes I think the soil will soften under me and I will sink out of sight. The vegetation clasps at the body too, not just to embrace it but to add it into its many folds and layers.

We take turns to sleep as a cautionary measure. I have seen many faces in the trees. They are always smiling and inviting, which is and isn't the problem; what troubles me is that they are there in the first place. Bash Man Goady nearly fell over when I told him about them. He sees them too.

Dear Future,

Even here you are still before me. You were ahead when I lived in Ariel. Should I equate the two on the basis of your changed relationship to me in both instances? I do anyway. As a child whose future is no longer a guarantee of his existence, I am allowed one or two pronouncements.

One, my present *is* my future. Two, my future is there, will always be there, to be lived. Three, another soul can live that future on my behalf so long as I approve. That's all.

I am tempted to raise these matters with Bash Man Goady and spend the next several moments in this ever-present in contented dispute with him. No, that would only distract us from our grander purpose of how to construct a slingshot. I'll talk to those friendly faces in the trees.

Dear Future,

Bash Man Goady, the genius, may have solved our mud-ball problem. Our attention was taken up with finding a way to get this loose soil to work like clay. There is a fruit here with a small round seed which is too slippery when fresh, but which when dry is still perfectly round and hard as a rock (there are no rocks here).

We've taken a sudden liking to this fruit, consuming a sickening amount (no sickness here). The seeds are lined up in the open out of reach of the soil.

The slingshot puzzle might prove insoluble. Time, or its equivalent here, will tell.

Dear Future,

We've laboured for an age to find material for a slingshot, spurred on by a hasty belief that because of the mud-ball solution, we were near. I have breathed, eaten, slept and conjured slingshot. Bash Man Goady has conducted himself with a new-found confidence. I am glad he was the one who hit on those seeds for pellets. Now it is incumbent upon me to find us a slingshot.

He stormed up to me with his hands glued to that stick of mine. Apparently he was testing various bits of wood for their strength when he gripped my ineffective bird trap. I told him the stick must have flown to that spot from one of the gum trees nearby.

'Sure it flew, launched by your fast hands.'

We used soil to remove the glue, water to remove the soil, then a gentle breeze dried his hands, helped by his flapping them about.

I think he really wants to find a slingshot so that he can say he solved both problems without my interference. I should let him, but I badly want to find it too. Somehow we've convinced ourselves that the slingshot is the more important of the two. Not to take anything away from Bash Man Goady's glory, but it is . . .

Dear Future,

Have I forgotten my family on account of my recent obsession with this slingshot business? No way. I think about them always. Have you given them a sign of my continued place in their lives? You are what you are with your own design and who am I to dictate anything to you? Yet I feel you owe me this one little thing because you are, in part, to blame for my present misery since I have no way of getting to you.

I have no sense of time here in this present. We sleep when we are tired. We talk about a future mostly as a reminder of what is not ours any longer, not even as a promise.

In talking about you, does that entitle us to a present that passes, however imperceptibly?

I was looking at my palm, my spread fingers, and suddenly saw all these forks in my hand, which would make ideal slingshots. I told Bash Man Goady. He was about to brush off the whole thing as ludicrous with that laugh of his, when he stopped and examined his hand, then jumped up and hugged me, calling me a genius. I started to get excited too and he said, 'Not really.' And before I complained, he followed that with, 'Bone. Bone will be our slingshot.' Does that mean we have solved this thing together? He seems to think so. The problem is how to find bone in a land where there are no dead.

Dear Future,

If I am dead and still able to talk to you, does that make you as unreal a prospect as me? Bash Man Goady believes this is the case. He has linked our slingshot enterprise directly to our means out of here. He is obsessed to the point of becoming unpleasant company.

There are two bones in my forearm. They are of unequal width but work equally well alongside each other. I tell him this and he laughs one of those long disdainful laughs reserved for when he wishes to register absurdity to the nth degree. I joined in with my breathy laugh. Then he started pointing at my forearm and slapping his thighs and laughing really hard. His antics tickled me. I pretended to launch a mud ball from my forearm. Soon we were on the ground, rolling, clutching our stomachs and begging each other with our watery eyes to stop.

Dear Future,

I am considering calling off this whole arrangement on account of your stubborn silence. Don't imagine that I am not aware that all this may be a test of my stoicism. I am not a fool. I was hit with the back of an axe and death stepped up to carry me away and I fought him off single-handed.

Life took my mother and three brothers from me and I put up with what I had left, my elder brother, and lived that life. You should know, dear future, that I laboured on in the belief that I would see them again. You should remember that without this belief I would have walked out into the middle of the red sand road when a convoy was passing the house and disappeared in a sandstorm under axle after axle.

Grant me this simple thing. You don't even do me the honour of saying 'No.' Instead you do what everyone with power over me (because I love them) has done to me up to now: kept me waiting in silence. This is not me about to give up. No way. You owe me this one thing since you are a right that has been denied to me. You know that. Work this one little thing for me. Let me know that you have given my people a sign of my continued existence. Not just mine, Bash Man Goady's too. We are a team, more than ever. We are becoming twins. At times one of us will tell the other what he is thinking as he is thinking it. Is this paradise playing tricks on us?

Dear Future,

Am I mistaken about you? Am I wrong to pour all my hopes into you? Should I devote every waking moment to finding a route or means out of here? My brother says there is not a second when he doesn't think about seeing everyone again. I doubted him. Then we got into an argument. I identified instances when I felt he was absorbed with more trivial matters. He tried to prove that very instance was an example of his devotion to getting us out of here. It ran for hours until I said this self same argument was proof that he was capable of being distracted. But he said the subject itself confirmed his argument.

'Leaving is not the same as trying to find a way to leave.'

'In my books worrying about something is as good as doing it.'

'In that case you should be satisfied with simply *thinking* about reuniting with Mother, Shick-shank, Big Forehead and Bellows.'

I'm sure he was about to hit me. He said, 'I love you.' I was ready to hit him back but I found myself saying, 'I love you too.' The trees were smiling.